CHRONICLES
OF THE
RED KING
The Secret Kingdom

CHRONICLES
OF THE
RED KING
The Secret Kingdom

JENNY NIMMO

SCHOLASTIC PRESS / NEW YORK

Library of Congress Cataloging-in-Publication Data

Nimmo, Jenny.
The secret kingdom / by Jenny Nimmo. — 1st ed.
p. cm. — (Chronicles of the red king ; 1)
Summary: Timoken and his sister, Zobayda, under the protection of a forest jinni but pursued by evil
viridees, straddle the world of men and the world of enchantments seeking a home while remaining young
by drinking a potion called Alixir.
ISBN 978-0-439-84673-8
[1. Magic — Fiction. 2. Brothers and sisters — Fiction. 3. Voyages and travels — Fiction.
4. Camels — Fiction.] I. Title.
PZ7.N5897Sec 2011
[Fic] — dc22
2010035710

10 9 8 7 6 5 4 3 2 1   11 12 13 14 15

Printed in the U.S.A.   23

First edition, June 2011

Book design by Elizabeth B. Parisi and Kristina Iulo

For Rhiannon, with love

CONTENTS

PROLOGUE

My name is Charlie Bone. I am thirteen years old and I live in a city in Britain that was built by my ancestor, an African king.

I have always wondered about the man known as the Red King. He was a magician, I was told, and he wore a red cloak. But no one seemed to know why he had traveled so far from his own country.

When I was ten something happened to me. Something odd. I began to hear the voices of people in photographs. Some of the people were already dead. The next phase of my peculiar "endowment" began when I looked at an old painting of a sorcerer. This time I not only heard him, I traveled right into his dingy old cell, all the way back into the sixteenth century. My grandmother told me I had inherited my endowment from the Red King, and I was sent to Bloor's Academy, a school for weekly boarders.

The Academy was run by a weird old man called Ezekiel Bloor. He was a hundred years old and a sort of magician. He was also descended from the Red King, and so were some of the students I met at the school. There were twelve of us who were known as the endowed.

In the past year there have been a lot of changes in the Academy. But we endowed still do our homework in the King's room. And the Red King's portrait still hangs in the space between the bookshelves. The paint has cracked and the king's face is shadowy and blurred, but there is a kind of light in his eyes, and I know that he is there, waiting for me.

It was my great-uncle Paton who suggested I help with the writing of this book. He had just finished reading the journals of our distant cousin, Bartholomew Bloor. Bartholomew is an explorer, and when he was traveling through Africa, he heard an ancient story about a boy and a flying camel. The same story cropped up again in Egypt. Bartholomew was intrigued. After that, wherever he went, he would ask questions about the boy and his camel. He was amazed to find the same story in Greece and Turkey and in cities all around the Mediterranean Sea. Often he was shown the caves and walls where carvings had been found, among them the image of a boy on a flying camel, as if it were a kind of signature.

Bartholomew began to draw maps so that he could revisit the places where he had heard the stories. Sometimes, when he asked about the boy and the camel, people's answers surprised him. In fact, the dates he was given for some of the sightings made no sense at all. If they were accurate, then the boy had not aged in two hundred years, nor had the camel.

In a lonely tavern in the Pyrenees, Bartholomew had the first inkling that he had stumbled on a story that was directly related to him. The innkeeper heard the tale from his great-grandmother, who knew everything about the village and its past. "There was a camel, certainly," he said, "and it could fly, no doubt about that. The boy would not be remembered, would he, if it had not been for the camel?"

An old woman sitting in a corner piped up, "Not true. Of course the boy would be remembered. He was a magician. An African king. He could bring rain and thunder; he could talk to animals. In that red cloak of his, he could do almost anything."

An African king? A magician in a red cloak? Bartholomew said that his heart missed a beat. He suddenly realized that, quite by chance, he had been following in the footsteps of his very own ancestor, the Red King.

The summer holidays had just begun when Uncle Paton called me. "It's about our ancestor, Charlie — the book I'm writing. Can you pop up to the shop this morning?"

The shop was Ingledew's Bookshop. Uncle Paton lived there with his wife, Julia, and Emma, her niece. They sold secondhand books, some of them very old and rare. The perfect place for a writer. My uncle was in the little room behind the shop. He was sitting at a desk piled high with ancient leather-bound books.

Uncle Paton is exceptionally tall, but I could only just see the top of his head poking up behind them.

"Charlie," he said. "Come and have a look at this."

The sofa was heaped up with books and papers as usual, but we pushed them to one side and sat down. Uncle Paton spread Bartholomew's maps across his knees. "Look," he said. "Look at the places marked with a cross. There are carvings there, pictures the Red King drew maybe nine hundred years ago."

"Yes," I said, sort of unsurprised. I had already seen the maps.

"Suppose you were to go and see them, Charlie. Suppose you found yourself traveling into them, suppose . . ."

"Suppose I were to meet him, when he was young?" I was so excited I jumped off the sofa. I'd already met the king when he was older. But the portrait in the school was painted at a time when the king was in mourning. He was pleased to see me, but never said much about his past. Now, at last, I might get a chance to find out who he really was and why he'd come to Britain.

Uncle Paton grinned. "You've got the idea, Charlie. You see those tomes"—he pointed to the books on the desk—"they might have been written hundreds of years ago, but they could have got a few things wrong. They can only tell us that the king arrived from Africa in the thirteenth century, that he was a magician, and married the daughter of a knight from Toledo. I want this book to be as truthful as I can make it. Bartholomew's journals are invaluable, of course, especially the maps. But we don't know what happened right at the very beginning, and why the king came so far."

"And we don't know what he thought and if his cloak was really magic?"

"The cloak. Hmm." Uncle Paton scratched his head. "We need Gabriel."

Gabriel Silk is a friend of mine. Another of the endowed. He's a bit odd — he lives with fifty-six gerbils and other assorted pets. But his family still possesses the Red King's cloak. Gabriel has incredible psychic powers. I knew what Uncle Paton was thinking. Wearing the cloak, Gabriel could use his ability to reach into the life of the Red King. Perhaps he could even see the world as the king saw it; he could listen, watch, and feel as he did.

As I said, it was the beginning of the summer holidays. We hadn't planned to go anywhere. Mom wasn't too keen on traveling; we'd just moved into a new house and there was still lots to do. But my dad was up for it. "Two weeks, Charlie. That's all I can spare for now, but we could always go again — in the autumn perhaps."

"And again and again and again?" I said.

My dad laughed. "Maybe, Charlie."

So my dad and I went to Africa. It was the best holiday I'd ever had in my life. We found the caves that Bartholomew mentioned. We found the rocks and walls and underground passages marked on his maps. We saw the pictures, the mysterious lines and shapes that the Red King had carved. And when I touched them, I met the boy who made them. And every time we met, the king's voice became clearer and his face brighter, until it seemed as if I was just talking to a friend who was sitting beside me. Little by little he told me his story, and with Gabriel's help, my uncle and I learned about the enchanted cloak, where it came from, and how it helped the king to become a marvelous magician.

This is the first book that Uncle Paton wrote about the Red King. As for the next one — that's another story.

CHARLIE BONE
Diamond Corner

CHAPTER 1
The Forest-Jinni

There was once a secret kingdom. It was hidden from the world by a forest as wide and as deep as a sea. The people who lived there had never known war, but they had heard of it. Stories of terrible strife and cruelty in the outside world had been passed down from the ancestors who had founded the kingdom. And so, although the people had never fought a battle, they could imagine it. They kept their spears polished to a high degree, and they painted fierce animals on their stout wooden shields. They even posted a watch in the tall towers that stood at each of the four corners of the palace.

The king was everything a king should be. Standing a head taller than most of his subjects, he was wise and just and dignified. He favored brightly colored robes and golden jewelry, which he wore looped in long ropes around his neck and in wide bracelets on his arms. Yet the crown he wore was a slim gold band, almost hidden in his thick black hair. It was a thousand years old and had once adorned the head of the first ruler of the secret kingdom.

The queen was a mystery. She was a very quiet woman, given to dreaming. It was believed that the king had chosen her for her exceptional beauty, but this was only part of the truth. He loved her for her fine mind, her kindness, and the magical quality of her voice.

The king and queen had one child: Princess Zobayda, who was two years old. Another baby was on the way but, for some reason, the imminent birth of this second child filled the queen with anxiety. It was the hottest time of the year, and yet the queen could not stop shivering. All day she paced the palace, muttering to herself. At night she cried in her sleep and called out, "Save him! Save my son!"

The king begged his wife to tell him about her nightmares. What was it that she feared so much? She was strong and healthy. Their kingdom was safe, and he tried to give her everything that she wished for. Why was she so worried about a child who had not even been born?

The queen could not say. She forgot her dreams as soon as she woke up, and did not understand why she found herself eroding the patterns on the tiled floor with her endless pacing. She had worn out one hundred pairs of shoes and now went barefoot. Her feet were sore and blistered, and still she paced. Sometimes the king felt dizzy watching his restless wife.

One night, a great storm blew up. The wind raged across the secret kingdom, uprooting trees and sending rivers of water through the streets. Thunder roared endlessly and lightning flashed across the land, turning night into day.

The windows in the palace were shuttered and barred, and the king and queen sat close together on a low couch filled with gold-embroidered cushions. For once the queen was motionless. She listened to the wind, leaning slightly, as though she were hearing voices.

"What do they say?" asked the king, half in jest. He took his wife's hand. "Do they . . . ?" he began.

"Shh!" hissed his wife. "Something is coming!"

At that instant, the shutters cracked apart and something flew into the room. It lay facedown, its ragged wings spread against the marble floor. The wings were not feathered, but as fine and delicate as a moth's. They sprouted from the being's bony shoulders; dark, earth-colored wings with pearly veins. The rest of the body was covered in a grayish silk that, at first, appeared like a fine mist, but gradually settled around the stranger's body, revealing its puny form.

The royal couple stared at the creature as it slowly folded its wings and pulled itself into a kneeling position. Even the king was speechless.

The little being raised its head and gazed at the queen. It had mottled gray skin and huge saffron-colored eyes. Its long nose was narrow, the tip overhanging its thin gash of a mouth. Its tiny ears rested in cavities on either side of its head, and it had no hair at all.

In spite of the creature's disturbing features, the queen was not alarmed. "What has happened to you?" she asked gently.

The creature crawled toward the queen and grabbed the hem of her robe. "Forgive me," he said. "I had nowhere to go, nowhere at all. They pursue me everywhere."

"Who pursues you?" asked the king, a little roughly. "My people harm no one, even . . . even . . ."

"A jinni?"

"Indeed, a jinni, if that is what you are?"

"A forest-jinni." The creature's voice had an echo, a distant cascade of tiny bells that enchanted the queen. "There is only one of us . . . now." His frail wings drooped.

"You appear to be lost," said the queen. "How can we help you?"

"Lost, lost. I am lost." Two fat tears rolled down the jinni's mottled cheeks. "I flew above the forest. I dared not stop. For days and days I traveled through the air. I could hear them below me. They would not let me rest. And then the wind caught me. It hurled me into your beautiful kingdom—" The jinni paused and took a breath. "And now I am here. At Your Majesties' mercy." He bowed his head.

The king stroked his chin and glanced at his wife. The recent lines of weariness and apprehension had left her face.

"I shall tell a servant to prepare a bed for you," said the queen. "If, indeed, you are used to such things. And some food. What do you like to eat, forest-jinni?"

"Fruit?" said the jinni tentatively. More tears formed in the corners of his orange-yellow eyes, and he looked up at the colored tiles that patterned the ceiling above him. "I have not known kindness for so long, it bewilders me."

"Everyone deserves kindness," said the queen. "Without it, we would die."

The king rang a small bell placed on a table at his side, and a servant appeared. When the man saw the jinni, he gave a gasp of horror.

"We have a guest," the queen said firmly. "Bring us a tray of fruit and have a bed prepared for him. Treat our visitor exactly as you would treat me, with respect."

"Yes, Majesty." The servant blinked at the jinni and retreated.

That night the queen had her first peaceful sleep in months. The storm rolled away, and in the morning the kingdom was bathed in a gentle, sunlit mist.

When the queen went to see if the jinni was awake, she found him curled in the very center of the large bed. His wings were folded neatly behind him, and he appeared to be fast asleep. Realizing the creature must be very tired, the queen tip-toed away.

The jinni slept for three days. When he woke up, his wings had brightened and his mottled skin had taken on a healthy tinge of brown. He was given a large tray of fruit for breakfast and a cup of crystal-clear water.

After breakfast, the jinni announced that he must return to the forest. It was his home, and he must face whatever danger awaited him there.

"But it seems that they—whoever THEY are—will do you some terrible injury," said the queen. "Why else would you try so desperately to escape them? Do not leave us, forest-jinni. You can stay here for as long as you want."

The jinni shook his head. "They will never stop searching for me. Sooner or later they would come upon your peaceful kingdom and destroy it."

"Who?" the king asked, frowning. "Who are these creatures bent on destruction?"

"They are called viridees," replied the jinni. "They live deep in the forest, in the damp darkness that breeds rot and decay. They are sorcerers. They can take the shape of trees or plants or any green, growing thing, and they can live for two hundred years or more. There is great goodness in the forest; there is beauty and kindness." The jinni put his palms together, so that one hand lay on top of the other. "And then there is the other side." He turned his hands so that the upper hand lay underneath. "Where there is one, there is always its shadow."

The king and queen stared at the forest-jinni in horrified fascination, but, throwing his arms wide, the jinni said, "Don't despair. I will leave your kingdom before they can follow, and I shall give you my treasures."

"Your treasures?" said the king. Was it possible that treasures were hidden in those thin, misty garments?

The jinni looked eagerly at the queen, his eyes alight with excitement. "You are soon to have a child," he said. "It will be a boy, and you want him to be wonderful."

"Yes!" The queen clutched the edge of her seat and returned the jinni's earnest gaze. "But more than anything, I want him to be safe. I am so afraid for him. I do not know why. My fear is foolish . . . irrational."

"You can sense what might be," replied the jinni. "But I can change the future for you." From the floating folds of his robe he withdrew a length of fine, silvery gossamer. As he turned it in his hands, each tiny thread glittered with a different color. The queen caught her breath. She had never seen anything so magical.

"This was made by the last moon spider," said the jinni. "Never again will cobwebs like these adorn the forest. For the moon spiders have all gone. The evil ones realized, too late, that they had killed something that could have saved them."

"And will this protect our son?" asked the king. "He might not be the sort of boy who wants to wear a cobweb all his life."

"No need." The jinni smiled. "Wrap him in the web the moment he is born, and do not remove it until he smiles for the first time."

"Is that all?" the queen asked doubtfully. "And will he be protected from everything?"

"As long as he carries the web when he is in danger. But there is something else," the jinni said gleefully. "Your son will also be a marvelous magician. For I have splashed the web with the tears of creatures that have never been seen, and I have dipped it in dew caught on the petals of flowers that will soon disappear from the world" — he smiled, wistfully — "just like me, the last forest-jinni." He laid the shimmering silk on the queen's lap.

The queen stared at the web for a moment, unable to speak or to touch it. And then a thought occurred to her, and she said, "We have a daughter, Zobayda. Can you give her the same protection and the same gifts as our son?"

The jinni held the queen's gaze for several seconds. He appeared to be reading her future. "It is too late for Zobayda," he said at last. "A child must be touched by the web before two years have passed. But I have this." And from his garment he pulled a tiny sliver of silk. "Wind this around the princess's finger," he said, "and she will have magic at her fingertips."

It was the king who took the proffered silk from the jinni's slim hand, and as he did so, he was suddenly aware that the jinni was offering the last fragment of his own protection. The king looked at the queen and saw that she too was aware of the jinni's sacrifice. And yet, thinking of their daughter, neither of them could resist the gift. They accepted it without a word.

"There is one more thing," said the jinni and, like a conjurer, he pulled a bottle from his clothing. The glass was shaped like a bird, the liquid inside it as clear as water. The jinni told the king and queen that it was Alixir, the water of life. One drop, taken at every new moon, would halt the aging process.

No sooner had the queen taken the bottle than the jinni was gone, slipping out into the sky like a windblown leaf.

That night, while Zobayda was sleeping, the queen wrapped the piece of silk around her daughter's middle finger. Almost immediately it solidified into a beautiful silver ring. It was shaped like a wing and engraved with pearly veins. A little head could be seen, peeping out of the top, and a tiny foot protruded from the other end. It was the forest-jinni, made miniature and frozen into silver.

Before she went to bed, the queen put the moon spider's web into a deep chest. Beside it she placed the bottle of Alixir.

Three weeks later the royal baby was born. He had large, thoughtful eyes and a fine, sturdy frame. He did not make a sound when the queen wrapped him in the web. After five days, he pushed his little hands free of the silk and gave his mother a wide smile.

"A smile!" The queen lifted her baby out of his wrapping and dressed him in the scarlet robes that had been worn by generations of royal babies.

They named the baby boy Timoken, after the first ruler of the kingdom. As he grew, his parents watched him for signs of the magical gifts he was supposed to display. But Timoken seemed to be just like any other boy. Perhaps he was unusual in that he could watch falling rain for many hours, that he was entranced by dew-filled leaves, that he touched even tiny creatures with reverence, and that he listened to birdsong with a rapturous expression. When Timoken turned nine, his father gave him a pearl-handled knife. It was meant as a protection against snakes and scorpions, but Timoken often used it to carve pictures on the rocks. He could be mischievous, and he made friends easily. More than anyone else, it was his sister, Zobayda, whose company he most enjoyed. It pleased the king and queen to see their children so devoted to each other. "They will never be alone," the queen sighed happily.

Zobayda's silver ring never became too small for her. As she grew, it always fitted her finger perfectly. The queen told her that a magic being had given it to her, and that it would keep Zobayda safe forever. But the forest-jinni had never made that promise.

Meanwhile, the jinni had returned to the forest. He had nowhere else to go.

It was not long before the viridees found him. He was sitting by a pool and singing to himself. He had been expecting them.

Slowly they began to surround him. But where was the moon spider's web? They had watched from the shadows as the forest-jinni washed the web with the tears of rare creatures. They had observed the dipping of the web into dew caught in precious flowers, and they had glimpsed the bottle shaped like a bird. The jinni had filled the bottle from a pool of moonlit water, and the viridees had listened as the jinni cast a spell. But he had spoken too fast for them to understand or remember what he said.

The viridees guessed that the web was more amazing, more precious, and more powerful than anything they possessed. Of course, they wanted it. Their lord demanded it.

"Where is the web of the last moon spider?" The gurgling tone of a viridee stopped the jinni's song.

"You killed the last moon spider," said the jinni.

"What have you done with the web?"

The jinni shook his head. "You will never find it."

The viridees threw a net of creepers over the little creature. He did not resist. They took him to Degal, lord of the viridees, in his gloomy palace under the forest floor. The great hall was lit by the phosphorescent gleam of a thousand stalactites, and Degal sat on a throne carved from black marble and inset with emeralds.

"Where is it?" Lord Degal's voice burbled like the water in a deep cavern. "Where is the web of the last moon spider?"

The forest-jinni wriggled free of the net of creepers. He spread his wings as though he were about to fly, and he said, "In a place that you will never find."

Lord Degal's red eyes flashed. Pointing his rootlike finger at the forest-jinni, he cried, "You will show us where it is, or suffer unbearable tortures."

The forest-jinni hardly flinched. In his sweet, clear voice, he declared, "I am one with the web of the last moon spider. I am one with the ring made of spider silk. I am one with the boy who will live forever." Then he flapped his delicate wings and vanished.

When Timoken was eleven years old, the unthinkable happened. The secret kingdom was invaded. Ever since the forest-jinni had disappeared from their midst, the viridees had been searching for the moon spider's web and the bird-shaped bottle. Lord Degal formed an alliance with a bloodthirsty tribe from the East. In return for their help in finding the web, he promised them untold wealth and any kingdom that, together, they might defeat. And so began years of terror as small kingdoms were invaded and crushed by the murderous tribe and the powerful sorcery of the viridees.

Like a tide of darkness, Lord Degal's army emerged from the forest beyond the secret kingdom. The viridees and the tribal soldiers were dressed alike in black turbans and black tunics. They carried long, shining sabers, and their drums and horns drowned out every sound except for the trumpeting of their massive elephants. The people who lived on the outskirts of the kingdom were the first to fall beneath the long sabers. Those who survived fled, screaming, toward the palace. Behind them their houses burned and their families died.

Timoken and Zobayda heard the thunder of the advancing army. They ran up to the palace roof and saw the fires and the dark forms rushing toward them from every side.

The massive palace doors were closed and barred. Soon, a roaring crowd surrounded the building. Inside, all was silent. The king was pondering. For the first time in his life he did not know what to do. But there was only one way out of this dire situation. He would have to offer his palace and his kingdom to the invaders. In return, they must allow his people to live in peace or leave the kingdom in safety.

The children watched their noble father ride out to talk with Lord Degal. The king wore a white robe and carried a banner of peace. Degal, in deepest green, looked like the king's shadow. A large green emerald glittered in Degal's turban, and his green sash lifted in the breeze as the two horses met.

A streak of light flashed in the air above the king's head. A second later he had toppled from his horse, his head severed by Degal's shining saber.

A deep wail from below told the children what their eyes could not believe. Their father was dead. They ran, screaming, to their mother.

When the people saw their fallen king, they rushed at the enemy, waving their spears. But they were hunters, not soldiers; they were no match for Degal's brutal army.

One of the king's guards found the golden crown, lying in the dust. As he picked it up, a soldier ran at him, waving a saber. But before he was cut down, the guard threw the crown to a friend. Another soldier leaped on that man, only to see the crown, once again, tossed through the air. And so it continued, the circle of gold flying above the roaring mass of bodies, caught and passed on, until it reached one of the queen's attendants, who took it to the queen.

Her eyes clouding with tears, the queen wiped the blood and the dust from the crown and put it on her son's black curls. But the king's head had been wide and splendid, and the crown was too big for Timoken. It began to slip down over his face. Seeing the problem, Zobayda stepped forward and lifted the crown above Timoken's ears. Then she closed her eyes and uttered mysterious words in her light, breathy voice. It was almost as if she were asking a question, unsure of herself and what to expect. Under her slim fingers, the crown began to fit itself to Timoken's head, and gradually he felt himself almost to be a king. Looking at his sister's closed eyes, he whispered, "You are a faerie."

"Yes," she replied. "I believe I am."

The queen quickly gathered together a few of her children's clothes. She put them in a large goatskin bag, and then she took the moon spider's web and the Alixir from the chest and handed them to her son.

"Take great care of these," said the queen. "The bottle contains Alixir. You must both take one drop every new moon, and you will stay as you are."

Did this mean that he would not grow? Timoken was reluctant to remain a child. He wanted to be a man as soon as he could. "I don't need the Alixir," he said, frowning at the bird-shaped bottle. "I wish to grow older."

"Not yet," advised his mother. "You might be an old man before you find your new kingdom."

"Will I find a new kingdom?" asked Timoken.

"I am certain that one day you will find a home," said the queen.

"And what is this?" asked Zobayda, touching the web. "It looks like a cobweb, but it's so beautiful. Is it magic?"

"Yes," said the queen. "There's so little time to explain, my children, but it was made by the last moon spider. Keep it with you, always." She thrust it into the bag with the Alixir. "Now hurry, hurry!"

Timoken slung the bag over his shoulder. He looked bewildered. "What now?" he asked.

"Now?" said the queen. "Now you must go." She hugged her children, kissed them good-bye, and told them to leave the palace. The warlord and his soldiers were already storming through the building.

"How can we escape?" cried Zobayda. "We are surrounded."

"Come with me." The queen led her children back up to the roof. The sun blazed above their heads. Below them, the warlord's army stood in its own shadow.

"What now?" said Zobayda. "If we jump, we shall die."

"You will die if you stay, so you must fly." The queen's voice sounded almost triumphant.

Timoken sensed that his mother had been waiting a long time for this moment. "We can't fly," he said, bemused and afraid.

"I believe that you can," the queen told him, smiling. "Zobayda, put your arms around your brother and hold tight. Do not let go until you are safe."

"When shall we be safe?" begged Timoken. "Mother, what are you saying?"

"Do as I tell you," his mother commanded. "Look at the sun. Fly to it."

"I cannot," argued Timoken. "It hurts my eyes."

"Close them. Fly upward. Feel your way through the sky. You can do it, Timoken. Now!" The queen's voice began to crack with fear.

Timoken could hear soldiers running up the steps to the roof. Their weapons scraped against the walls and their rough voices echoed up the narrow stairwell. Timoken's heartbeat quickened. He could hardly breathe. Zobayda put her arms around his waist and held him tight.

"Now!" screamed the queen.

Timoken closed his eyes and turned his face up to the sun. Bending his knees a little he took a leap, just like he did when he was jumping from one of the fallen trees in the forest. Only this time he made himself believe that his feet would not touch the ground for a while. He found himself lifting into the air. The sun burned his face and he clung to his sister. They rose higher and higher.

"Timoken." He heard his mother's voice following him. "Timoken, keep your secret. Never tell . . . never let anyone know what you can do."

Timoken opened his eyes and looked down at the palace. His mother had disappeared in a sea of black. Soldiers covered the roof of the palace, their weapons glinting in the fierce sunlight.

"Zobayda, I can't see our mother!" cried Timoken.

Zobayda wouldn't look back. Tears streamed from her eyes and she buried her face in her brother's shoulder. "Mother," she murmured.

Timoken understood that they were now alone. Their lives had changed forever. But he could fly, and his sister had magic in her fingers. They would survive. He found that he could move through the air with no more than a thought in his head — a wishing.

CHAPTER 2
The Moon Spider's Web

The forest-jinni had not told the queen the whole truth. He was afraid that she would return the moon spider's web if she knew what might happen. He did not warn her that when a newborn baby had been wrapped in the web it would always have one foot in the world of men and the other in a realm of enchantments, a realm of good spirits and of others that were not so kind. Worst of all were the viridees.

As soon as Timoken left the kingdom, the viridees sensed that the web had left with him. They could smell it.

Unaware of the viridees and their malicious intent, Timoken and his sister floated through the vast sky, astonished to be so high above the earth, though their minds were clouded with the memory of their lost parents. Brother and sister could not bring themselves to speak. They drifted in silence, hour after hour, with no thought as to where they should go, or when they should touch the earth again. Their father had told them that every day the sun moved through the sky in an arc, from east to west. Beyond the African forest — north, east, and west — there was a vast desert where nothing could live. And in the south, where the sun reached its zenith, there was a world of water. Here things could live: birds, fish, and strange creatures as large as a palace.

Timoken saw that the sun was now low in the west, and so he wished himself south where, already, the night clouds were rolling in. Zobayda was so weary her arms were beginning to loosen around Timoken's waist. He had to clutch her tight, but his eyelids were drooping and he longed to close them.

Down, Timoken thought, *I must go down.* Immediately he found himself falling through the air. He could hear waves breaking below him; he could sense the swirl of a great body of water and felt something utterly unfamiliar: a cold dampness rising up to claim him. Zobayda's feet touched the water first, and she woke up.

"Timoken!" Zobayda screamed. "Leave here! Whatever lies below will kill us." She could feel icy claws clutching at her heels.

Timoken wished himself away from the fearful world of water. He felt his feet skimming the surface of the sea, but he could not rise above it. The claws were now clinging hungrily to his feet. The cold made his head spin and he could not fly anymore.

"I cannot fly!" Timoken moaned.

"You must," cried his sister. "Timoken, you MUST fly!"

Zobayda's desperate voice roused Timoken. He knew he must make an extra effort. With all the strength left in his weary head, he willed himself away from the water. There was a deep gurgle, a furious groan, and the icy claws slowly released their grip. Below the surface of the water, two giant crabs sank to the bottom of the sea.

Timoken and his sister floated across the waves until their feet touched a bank of sand. Timoken gave a happy sigh and let himself fall onto dry land. Zobayda rolled beside him and, holding hands, they fell fast asleep.

The children had fallen onto sand that was still warm from the sun. But, as midnight approached, the air began to freeze and the earth became colder and colder. The children woke up, shivering. They had left the secret kingdom in thin clothing, and had brought nothing to protect them from the cold.

Timoken frantically pulled clothes from the goatskin bag. Every garment was made of fiber spun to a fine silk. When the queen packed the bag she had been too distressed to think of chilly nights. At last, Timoken came to the moon spider's web. To his cold hand the web felt warm and comforting. He shook it out. A huge net of sparkling strands unfurled in the air. It fell softly over the children and covered them like a blanket.

"Our mother said it was magic," said Zobayda.

Timoken regarded the gleaming folds of the web. In the very center, where the threads formed a tight net, he glimpsed an extraordinary face. It had huge saffron-colored eyes, a long nose, and a thin mouth that seemed to be smiling.

"What are you?" asked Timoken, in a whisper.

"I am the last forest-jinni," said a voice with a musical echo. "And you are my creation. Believe in yourself, Timoken. Your road is long and perilous, but keep me safe and you will survive. My gifts are many."

"What are you staring at?" asked Zobayda, sleepily. She moved her legs beneath the web and the yellow eyes wavered, then the small face vanished.

Before Timoken could explain what he had seen, he became aware that they were being watched. The sand behind them slithered and crunched and, all at once, the children were surrounded. A group of warriors stood staring down at the children. Their painted spears glistened in the moonlight, but their faces were shadowed by tall feathered hats. Timoken could see their eyes, eyes that were fearful and amazed.

The men began to murmur to one another. At first, Timoken could not understand them, and then he began to make sense of their strange, mumbled language.

"It hurts my eyes," said one.

"It burns my face," said another.

"I cannot breathe," gasped a third.

The men began to back away, but one pointed his spear toward the children. They screamed and, instinctively, pulled the web up to their chins. The man gave a savage snort and brought his spear closer to their faces. Timoken's heart hammered in his chest; he waited for the weapon to slice through his neck. But as soon as the spear touched the web, there was a bright flash. The warrior screamed in pain and leaped away, dropping his spear. "Devil children," he hissed.

At this, the group let out a wail of terror and fled. The children could hear their feet stumbling over the deep sand until they were swallowed by the great silence of the desert night.

"The web saved our lives," said Zobayda, gazing at the shining coverlet of spider silk.

"We will always be safe," said Timoken, laying his head on the sand.

This time the children slept long and deeply. They awoke to find themselves in a strange landscape of huge, rolling sand dunes. Timoken ran to the top of a dune and looked out. On every side, the desert stretched in golden folds until it reached the horizon. Nothing moved. There was not a blade of grass, not a tree, and not even the hint of a stream. The warriors' footprints had been blown away by the wind, so there was no way of knowing where they had gone. Timoken plunged down the sand dune, stumbling, falling, and laughing as his feet sank into the deep sand.

Zobayda had found food in the goatskin bag: dried fruit and meat, beans, and millet cakes. But there was nothing to drink.

"Perhaps we'll find a stream," said Timoken, "or perhaps it will rain." He chose to ignore what his father had told him — that nothing could live in the desert.

They were careful not to finish the food. It might have to last for many days. Zobayda wrapped what was left in the moon spider's web; today the web felt cool, in spite of the burning heat.

They had no idea which way to go. Zobayda suggested they fly. From high above the earth they would have a better view, and would surely see a village or a stream, or even a forest.

Timoken slung the bag over his shoulder, and Zobayda hugged his waist. Then Timoken bent his knees a little and leaped from the sand. Up and up and up. He flew north for a while, but when he looked down there was still nothing but desert far below him. He flew west and east, only to see the same barren landscape stretching on and on for miles. The heat in the upper air was making him dizzy. He could feel the skin on his face burning up. Timoken let himself fall back to earth, but before his feet touched the ground, a great bird swooped out of the sky. Its huge talons sank into Timoken's shoulders, and it began to shake him.

Timoken nearly fainted with the pain. He could hear his sister's voice, screaming at him. "The web, Timoken. Use the web!"

He put his hand into the bag, but as his fingers found the web, a voice in his head told him, *No, no, no. That's what they want. The bird will steal it.*

"The web!" Zobayda screamed again. "It will protect us!" She slid her fingers around Timoken's waist, reaching for the bag. But Timoken slapped her hand away, crying, "No, Zobayda. Not this time. The bird will steal it."

"The bird will kill us," yelled Zobayda. "What else can we do?"

"Use your fingers," Timoken croaked, weak with pain. He knew he would soon lose consciousness.

"My fingers," Zobayda murmured. Clinging to her brother with one arm, she stuck her ringed finger into the bird's feathered underside. As she did this, she chanted:

> *Shrivel wing.*
> *Flap and spin.*
> *Wither beak.*
> *Shrink and squeak.*

With a deafening screech, the bird let go of Timoken's shoulders. He opened his eyes just wide enough to see a small feathered thing, no bigger than a mouse, spinning toward the earth.

"It worked," cried Zobayda, amazed by the success of her ringed finger.

"Just in time," her brother grunted as they plummeted to earth. Distracted by the pain in his shoulders, he lost control of his flying, and they landed on the sand with an uncomfortable bump.

Zobayda sat up and held out her fingers. A tiny yellow eye, set into the silver ring, blinked at her.

"Oh!" Zobayda jumped. "The creature on my ring — it blinked."

Timoken peered at the silver wing wrapped around his sister's finger, and at the tiny head peeping above it. "Did our mother tell you about the ring?" he asked.

"She said it would keep me safe," said Zobayda.

"It is an image of the last forest-jinni," Timoken told her. "I saw him in the web."

Before they could even think of moving again they ate some dried fruit, hoping to soothe their aching throats. After their snack, they took a pair of thin tunics from the goatskin bag and wrapped them around their heads. With their heads covered, Timoken and Zobayda struck north, away from the pitiless sun. They knew, now, that they were surrounded by thousands of miles of dead earth. And yet the warriors had come from somewhere. Perhaps they lived in caves beneath the sand? Perhaps, somewhere, there were other caves, uninhabited, where fresh water dripped from the rocks, and where they could find shelter from the withering heat.

It was not long before Zobayda sank onto her knees, crying, "I am dying of thirst, Timoken. What can we do?"

Timoken's throat was so parched, he could barely reply. Did it never rain in the desert? Did the white clouds passing high above them never consider travelers in the desert, never allow a few of their millions of droplets to fall? *We shall die*, thought Timoken, *if something does not happen.*

Perhaps it was this moment that set the course of Timoken's life. He found that he could not give in. It would have been easy to lie in the sand and never wake up. But the forest-jinni had told him to believe in himself. And so he would. Human beings did not fly, but he did. What else might he be capable of? He took the moon spider's web from the goatskin bag and spread it on the ground.

"What are you doing?" croaked Zobayda. "Save your strength."

Timoken picked up a corner of the web and turned on his heel. Around and around he spun, faster and faster. The web flew out in the torrid air and a tiny breeze fanned Zobayda's cheeks. She sat up and watched her brother. How could he whirl so fast in this heat? Timoken had become a spinning pillar, the web a circling wheel of silver.

Second by second the air became fresher. Zobayda stood and held out her hands. She could feel the breeze sweeping over her hot fingers and she closed her eyes, savoring its coolness. The air was filled with a soft humming. Was it the web stirring the air, or her brother's voice?

Something touched Zobayda's upturned hand: a light droplet, and then, another. She opened her eyes. Rain fell on her head and slid down her cheeks. It splashed her blue robe and trickled into her shoes. She threw back her head and let the rain splatter into her mouth. "Timoken!" she gurgled. "You are a magician."

Laughter came flying out of the whirling figure. "Save the water, Zobayda. I can't keep spinning forever."

Zobayda emptied the goatskin bag, scattering its contents on the sand. She opened the bag as wide as she could and let the rain tumble into it. When it was half-full, she called to her brother, "Stop, Timoken, before you turn into a pillar. We have enough water for days and days. Besides, I am getting very wet."

Timoken sank to the ground. The rain thinned and pattered, and then it stopped. Timoken lay staring up at the blue sky. "I burst the clouds," he said, laughing delightedly.

Zobayda tied their belongings in a long crimson robe that their mother had packed. She put the parcel on her head and balanced it with her hand. "You can carry the water," she told Timoken.

The goatskin bag was now very heavy. Timoken tried carrying it on his head but the water slopped about uncomfortably. He would have to use his arms. Once again they headed north. After a while, a range of mountains appeared, a wavering line of blue on the far horizon.

The rain had woken hundreds of creatures that had been sleeping beneath the dry sand. Lizards scurried over the children's feet, snakes slithered around boulders, and insects of every size and color appeared in the sky. They flew in a haze around the children's heads, buzzing and clicking. The desert was no longer dead.

Small, mouselike creatures popped their heads out of the sand. They watched the children, their black eyes round with astonishment. One of them squeaked, and Timoken had a feeling that he understood the creature. He stopped, put down the water bag, and stared at the furry head.

"Timoken, come on!" called his sister. "Those ratty things are not going to tell you anything."

On the contrary, thought Timoken. He smiled at the creature, and its expression seemed to soften. It pulled itself right out of the sand and, sitting on its hind legs, it said, "Safe journey!" Or did it?

"Thank you," said Timoken.

"Timoken!"

Zobayda was now a good way ahead of her brother. But what was the use of hurrying, when you didn't know where you were going? There might be more to be gained by talking to someone — or something — that knew the desert.

Timoken knelt beside the creature. It gazed at him in a friendly way. Its companions were emerging from the sand. They turned their heads to look at Timoken, and sniffed the air with interest.

Timoken cleared his throat and asked, "What are you?" He was surprised to hear his words emerge from his throat in a series of soft squeaks.

"We are us," said the creature.

There was no doubt about what it had said. Timoken could understand its language.

"Other things call us sand-rats," the creature went on.

"Sand-rats," Timoken repeated. "I am human. My name is Timoken." He pointed at Zobayda, who was resolutely plowing ahead. "And that is my sister."

The sand-rat looked at Zobayda. "She goes the wrong way," it said. "Do not follow."

Timoken frowned. "The wrong way? How can you tell?"

"There are bad spirits that way," squeaked the sand-rat. "Viridees."

"VIRIDEES!" echoed the other sand-rats, and suddenly they were gone. All that remained were several small mounds of sand.

"Stop, Zobayda!" called Timoken. "You are going the wrong way."

"How do you know?" she called back.

"The sand-rat told me."

Zobayda stopped. She turned and stared at her brother. "That can't be true."

"It is, Zobayda."

Timoken's sister walked toward him, slowly. "You mean you could understand their language?"

Timoken nodded. "And I could speak it. They told me that there are bad spirits the way you were going. They called them viridees."

He watched the disbelief on his sister's face turn to astonishment. "You really can talk to animals," she said, her eyes wide with awe. "What else can you do, Timoken?"

"Who knows?" Timoken grinned. He picked up the goatskin bag and balanced it firmly on his head. "Let's go east," he said, with confidence.

Zobayda saw a pale semicircle beginning to rise above the eastern dunes. She fell into step beside her brother and together they walked toward the moon.

The light had almost left the sky when they saw the THING — a dark shape on the horizon. It wavered and grew in size as it approached them. Zobayda's instinct was to turn and run, but Timoken clutched her hand, saying, "It will catch us, and then we will be too tired to fight. Besides . . ."

"Besides?" asked Zobayda.

"We do not know what it is."

They stood and waited, while the thing drew nearer. Now they could make out huge teeth, bulging eyes, and great galloping feet. It began to make a noise, a long, snorting bellow, like a creature from the underworld.

Zobayda crumpled to her knees, crying, "We should have run!"

CHAPTER 3
Sandstorm

It was a camel, an animal that Timoken had seen painted on the walls of the palace courtyard, but never in the flesh. The huge animal appeared to be angry. It was making straight for the children, its head tossing from side to side and its deafening bellows increasing as it approached. Long strands of spittle hung from its lower jaw — and those teeth! Those feet!

"Get up, Zobayda," hissed Timoken, "or you'll be trampled. We have to face this creature." He lowered the water bag to the ground and grabbed his sister's hand, pulling her to her feet.

The camel slowed its pace. It gave a throaty bleat and stepped toward the children. Zobayda peeped from behind her hand and shivered.

"Good day!" Timoken's greeting emerged as a soft version of the camel's bleat.

The camel blinked. "Gabar!" it snorted.

"Gabar," Timoken repeated. *Possibly the camel's name,* he thought.

The camel blinked again, its long, curling eyelashes fluttering like birds' wings.

Zobayda forced herself to look up at the camel's face. Compared to a horse, this creature was ugly.

Timoken noticed that an odd sort of saddle rested on the camel's hump. It was made of intricately carved wood and looked like a shallow cradle. Inside the cradle there were brightly colored cushions braided in gold and silver. The camel's harness was made of plaited leather joined with rings of gold and hung with tiny bells, and its saddle was weighted by heavy bags. So where was the camel's wealthy owner?

"Where is your master?" Timoken asked the camel.

The animal remained silent.

"Is he dead?" asked Timoken.

The camel turned its head so that one eye looked at the boy suspiciously. Timoken felt uncomfortable. If a sand-rat could understand him, why not a camel?

"Perhaps we could ride it," Zobayda suggested. "It has fine feet for walking over the sand."

How could they climb up to the camel's lofty hump? The animal was obviously in no mood to help them. It gave a long bleat and walked around the children, heading west, away from the moon.

But the moon had vanished and a dark cloud was beginning to fill the sky: a cloud that grew every second, a cloud that filled their ears with its roar and sent a torrent of sand bowling toward them across the desert floor.

"A sandstorm!" cried Zobayda. "Timoken, run!"

They ran in the camel's wake. It was galloping again, and bellowing fearfully. It had obviously been running from the sandstorm until the children had, momentarily, held it up.

The great cloud of sand was almost upon them when the camel suddenly stopped. "Behind me!" it snorted.

Timoken grabbed his sister's hand, and they stumbled to the camel. By the time they reached him, the air was thick with sand. They threw themselves onto the ground behind the great creature, and he sank to his knees. Flying sand thundered about them, stinging their eyes, filling their noses, and coating their hair.

Timoken could feel his sister struggling with her bundle of clothes. Something cool and soft touched his face, and then covered his head. *The web*, he thought.

Holding the web before her, Zobayda stood up and faced the storm. The sand rushed past the web, never touching her. Slowly, she pulled one end of the web over the camel's head, tying a corner to his harness. Only then did she duck down, bringing the other end of the web over herself and her brother.

"That was brave," Timoken whispered, still hardly daring to open his mouth.

"I had to cover the camel's face," she said, "or he would have drowned in sand."

Timoken looked up at the glittering threads above him. The sand was bouncing harmlessly off the web, as though the flimsy strands of silk were made of steel. *We're safe*, he thought drowsily. A moment before he fell asleep, he remembered that the camel had spoken.

"The camel spoke," he told his sister, "and I understood him."

Zobayda smiled. "He's not suspicious of us anymore."

All three slept. The windblown sand stormed over their heads, and the moon spider's web kept them safe and warm.

In the morning, when the children lifted the edge of the web, they saw that they were, in fact, in a hole. They were surrounded by a wall of sand. Timoken stood up. His head came to just above the top of the wall.

"We'd have been buried alive," said Zobayda, "without this." She gathered up the web, untying the corner from the camel's harness.

The camel got to his feet, grumbling and bellowing. Sand flew off his back as he shook his great head. The children worried that he would not be able to get out of the hole. But the camel set his great feet against the sloping side and climbed out with ease.

"Now us," said Timoken.

The children began to crawl their way upward, pushing the goatskin bag and the parcel of clothes before them. The wall crumbled beneath their hands and feet as they clawed and slid in the soft sand. And all the while the camel watched their progress with a superior expression; once or twice he almost seemed to smile.

It was a long time before the children finally stumbled out, dragging their possessions with them. They lay on their backs and closed their eyes against the bright sunlight, their limbs aching from the climb.

The camel suddenly gave a long, loud bellow. Timoken answered with a small sound of his own.

"What's going on?" Zobayda asked.

"He says we must move quickly," Timoken told her, "but I said we needed more time."

The camel bellowed again, and kicked up a cloud of sand. "No time," he said. "Must go. QUICK!"

"All right, all right," moaned Timoken, getting to his feet. "But we need a drink, and so do you, I'm sure."

The camel blinked. "Water? Where?"

Timoken carefully undid the goatskin bag. Water had seeped from the top, but there was still enough to drink for all three of them — depending on how much a camel needed.

Before they could stop him, the camel plunged his head into the bag and began gulping up the water in great, long drafts. A few more gulps and all the water would be gone. Timoken seized the camel's harness and tried to drag his head away. "Stop!" he cried. "You'll empty the bag, and we need a drink, too."

"Got to fill up," gurgled the camel.

"We saved your life with our magic web," Timoken protested. "This is a fine way to repay us."

The camel stepped away from the bag. He rolled his eyes and shook his head, jingling the bells on his harness. "Drink, magic children," he said, in an awestruck bleat.

Zobayda laughed. She could not understand the rumbling camel language, but she had a good idea what was going on.

When the children had sipped up the few handfuls of water that were left, Timoken tied the handles of the empty bag and slung it over his shoulder. The sun was rising fast, the heat burning their faces. He would have to bring on another rainstorm before long, but the camel was anxious to move, and how much easier it would be to travel on his back, rather than plowing over the sand or flying through the hot air. Besides, the animal seemed to know where he was going.

"Could we . . . ride on you?" Timoken asked, in what he thought was a polite sort of bleat.

"Naturally," said the camel.

Timoken stared up at the camel's hump, so far above him. "But how . . . ?"

The camel sank to his knees and grunted, "How do you think?"

The saddle looked safe and comfortable. The children climbed up and sat cross-legged among the cushions. Timoken took the reins that lay across the pommel at the front of the saddle. He gave them a little shake and the bells on the harness gave a silvery chime.

The camel got to his feet.

"Where are we going?" asked Timoken.

"No idea," came the rumbling reply.

"I thought you knew," muttered Timoken as the camel set off. Soon he was galloping. Zobayda wrapped her arms around her brother's waist while Timoken held tight to the pommel. The wooden saddle swung and bounced beneath them, and the shiny cushions slid this way and that.

After a while, a curious conversation between the boy and the camel began. Timoken learned that Gabar was indeed the camel's name. His master had been a wealthy merchant, crossing the desert to barter fine silk from the north with gold and jewels from the south.

"What happened?" asked Timoken, his voice wobbling from the jolting of the camel's long strides.

"Viridees!"

That name again. "What are viridees?"

A low rumble came from Gabar's throat. "Killers! Evil ones! They told Master to catch children. He said no. So they sent jackals to pull him off my back. They blew their foul breath in his face, and I was afraid. I ran. I am ashamed. But I knew he would die." Gabar groaned.

Timoken patted Gabar's shaggy neck. "You are not to blame."

"Next time I will not run away," said Gabar. "I was afraid when I met you, but you are my master now, and I will not let you die."

"We have no intention of dying," said Timoken. "I can perform enchantments, and my sister has magic in her fingers."

"That is why they want you," grunted Gabar.

"The viridees want US?" said Timoken.

"Both of you," said Gabar. "They search the desert. They sent the sandstorm. They killed my master. They will do anything to find you."

Timoken shuddered. He thought, *If the viridees want us, it is not only for what we can do, but what we have: the moon spider's web.*

Zobayda asked why Timoken and the camel had been bleating and grunting at each other. Timoken repeated what Gabar told him about the viridees.

"They want the web, Zobayda," said Timoken.

"And the Alixir," Zobayda reminded him. "Who would not want to live forever?"

CHAPTER 4
Voices in the Cave

Gabar carried the children to a range of mountains in the northern desert. Zobayda and Timoken were asleep, when the camel began to bellow and stamp his feet. They woke up with a start, rubbing their eyes and stretching their aching legs.

"Time to rest," grunted Gabar. He sank to his knees and the saddle tilted violently.

Luckily, Zobayda had wound a long scarf around herself and her brother, and tied the ends of the scarf to the saddle, so they would not fall out. Before they could climb down she had to untie the knots, but her fingers were stiff with cold, and she could not loosen them.

"Help me, Timoken," she demanded, "or we'll be tied to this camel forever."

Timoken was staring at the sky. Never had he seen so many stars. Their cold light fell across the desert, making the sand glitter like ice. Shivering, he helped his sister with the knots so they could climb off the camel's back.

Gabar had remembered a cave where his master used to rest. Here it was, tucked into the mountainside, a few steps up from the sand. The children clambered into the cave. Away from the chilly air, their shivering gradually subsided. Zobayda decided to unpack some of their food, but it was so dark she could not even see her own hands. Groping in her bundle she found a candle, but there was no fire to light it.

"You can bring rain; perhaps you can make fire," Zobayda said to her brother.

Timoken flexed his fingers. Making fire seemed a step too far. "It was your hand that touched my crown and made it fit," he said. "And your hand that saved us from the giant bird."

"Yes, but I don't think—"

"Try."

"Very well." Zobayda balanced the candle on the floor of the cave. She cupped the tip of the candle in her two hands and whispered to herself. Or was she speaking to the candle? Whatever the words she used, the thin string in the lump of wax refused to respond.

"My fingers are too cold," said Zobayda.

"Don't give up," urged Timoken.

His sister bent her head. A flutter of sound came from her, a quiet song. Her cupped fingers began to glow. "Oh!" She lifted her hands and revealed a tiny flame.

"You did it!" cried Timoken.

Zobayda seemed surprised by what she had done. As the flame grew, it filled the cave with light, and she could see her ring, sparkling as never before. She was certain the little face smiled at her.

"It was the ring," she told Timoken, "not my fingers."

Gabar's master had left piles of brushwood at the back of the cave, ready for his next visit. Timoken quickly gathered some up and lit a fire with the candle. Warmth spread through the children's bodies. Sitting close to the fire, they ate all the dried meat they had left. Now there were only millet cakes and beans. They wondered how long these would have to last.

There was a bag of grain behind the brushwood. For the camel, guessed Timoken. He carried it out to Gabar, who was sitting alone in the cold desert.

Gabar grunted his thanks and began to munch, while Timoken undid the saddle and lifted the heavy bags off the camel's back.

"In the morning, I will make rain," Timoken told Gabar, "and you will drink."

Gabar gave a snort. "Really?"

"You'll see," said Timoken. "Good night, Gabar."

Zobayda had spread a blanket of clothes on the cave floor and the children lay down, pulling the web on top of themselves. In no time at all they were asleep.

An hour later Timoken woke up. The fire was only a pile of embers, and its flickering light cast long shadows over the cave walls. As Timoken stared at the shadows he could see that they were, in fact, long, flowing lines. Were they letters, or pictures?

Timoken sat up. The shadows held voices. He stood and approached the wall. He touched the rough surface and felt the rock throb, as though it were alive.

"Who are you?" Timoken whispered.

A thousand voices rushed out at him. He couldn't tell one voice from another, there was such a babel of sound. He glanced at Zobayda, expecting her to leap up in fright. But she slept on, oblivious to the noise.

Gradually, Timoken began to make out the different voices. He found that he could listen to one and block out the rest. The owner of the first voice described a fine city where he lived with his wife and ten children; the next spoke of a market where gold and silver trinkets, exotic fruit, and rolls of cloth lay on tables, shaded from the sun by canopies of hide; another voice told of wolves in a dark forest; another of his escape from a giant sea creature that swallowed his boat.

Timoken realized that the voices belonged to travelers who had rested in the cave and written about their lives on the cave wall. Somehow the voices of those travelers had reached Timoken through the marks on the rock. He was excited by the notion that he could tell his own story to future travelers, and he took out the pearl-handled knife his father had given him and began to carve pictures into the rocky wall.

He had hardly begun his story when he became aware of another presence in the cave. Someone was watching him. He felt that the images he carved were spinning forward, traveling beyond him as he scrawled and scraped in the firelit cave. His spidery lines were reaching through the years; a message sent into the future to someone he would never know.

But suddenly there he was, staring out from the cave wall: a boy of thirteen or fourteen, with skin paler than Timoken's, and lively brown eyes. His dark hair was thick and unruly, his smile irresistible. Timoken smiled back.

The boy was wearing unusual clothing: a red garment stretched tight across his body, and dirty trousers of some rough blue material.

"There you are!" The boy's voice was so clear that Timoken had to take a step back. He found that he could understand the boy, even though he spoke a foreign language.

After a moment's hesitation, Timoken asked, "Who are you?"

What was that? Did the boy say "Charlee"? A difficult name. Timoken frowned. "Where are you?"

"I'm here," the boy replied. "I couldn't believe that this would happen."

"It is astonishing," Timoken agreed.

"I've tried so many times to reach you," the boy went on, "but always that other one has stopped me. Now, at last, he's gone."

"Who?"

"You must know. But then, perhaps you haven't met him yet. I can see that you are only ten or eleven years old."

"I am eleven," said Timoken. "Tell me, who is 'that other one'?"

"The shadow. Hark—"

A cry from Zobayda cut through the boy's next words.

"Timoken, you're talking to a wall," said Zobayda, rubbing her eyes. "Are you sleepwalking?"

"No," Timoken retorted, staring at the wall. The boy had disappeared. "I wish you hadn't done that."

"What?"

"You broke the link."

Zobayda yawned. "You're not making sense."

Timoken remained staring at the wall. He studied each line, hoping for the boy to return. But he never reappeared. At length, cold and shivering, Timoken slipped under the web and lay beside his sister. He wanted to tell her about the boy and the voices, but did not know how. He could not even begin to describe the emotion that had gripped him when he saw the boy's smiling face.

"What is it, Timoken?" murmured Zobayda. "Something is troubling you."

"I'm not troubled. I'm . . . I don't know. I heard voices coming from the cave wall, hundreds of them. And then I saw a boy. I think he is special to me. It sounds odd, and you probably don't believe me."

"I can believe almost anything of you, my brother," Zobayda mumbled sleepily.

In the morning, Timoken spun on the sand, whirling the web in the dawn air, and rain fell, just as he had predicted. The goat-skin bag was filled with water and offered to Gabar. The camel showed no surprise. He emptied the bag, belched, and asked for breakfast.

"I'm sure you've never seen anyone else bring rain like that?" Timoken said to the slightly ungrateful camel.

"You are a rare human," Gabar replied, munching his breakfast grain. "And that is that." The camel had obviously ceased to be amazed by human behavior.

Timoken heaved the heavy saddle onto the camel's back, but before they replaced the merchant's bags, Zobayda wanted to know what they contained. Opening the first bag they discovered dried fruit and meat, and more grain for the camel. The second bag was packed with rolls of silk; the third was by far the heaviest, and it was difficult to open. When the children finally managed to untie its leather strings, they found another bag inside it, and another inside that, and then a fourth.

The stiff leather hide cut their fingers, and Zobayda would have given up, but Timoken was, by now, impatient to find out what lay inside such well-protected bags. He used his pearl-handled knife to cut through the leather, and the last bag fell open. A long, carved-ivory chest was revealed, the lid secured with a golden clasp. Carefully, Timoken undid the clasp and lifted the lid.

The brightness that lay within the chest caused Zobayda to reel back with a gasp. Timoken gazed, unable to believe his eyes. The chest was filled with precious jewels: gold bangles, necklaces, strings of rubies and pearls, diamond rings, and emerald clasps all lay heaped together in a glittering mass.

"Gabar's master was more than a merchant," Timoken murmured. "He must have been a prince."

"We are rich," breathed Zobayda.

Why did the viridees ignore this chest? Timoken wondered. He asked the camel for his opinion.

"They don't need human treasure," Gabar replied.

"But they want what we have," said Timoken. "They want it so badly that they sent a sandstorm, and they killed your master for refusing to help them."

The camel grunted his agreement.

Zobayda took a handful of jewels from the chest before they closed it. "It will pay for our suppers when the food runs out," she said.

As long as we can find an honorable tradesman, thought Timoken.

With some difficulty, they managed to tie the chest into the three bags, but Timoken had cut the strings of the fourth, so they had to leave it open.

When all the bags were secured, the children climbed onto Gabar's back. Zobayda wrapped the scarf around herself and her brother, and tied the ends to the saddle. Timoken shook the reins and the camel stood up. It was up to him now. He had crossed the desert many times; he knew the trade routes. Timoken asked Gabar to take them to the nearest habitation.

"And what will you do there?" Gabar inquired.

Timoken did not know how to answer. "What will we do when we find a village, or a city?" he asked his sister.

Zobayda had no doubts. "If we like it, we shall make our home there."

"And if we don't like it?"

"Then we shall move on," Zobayda said cheerfully. "And one day we will find a home."

"But not a mother, not a father."

Zobayda was silent for a moment, and then she said quietly, "It's just you and me now, Timoken."

"And Gabar," said her brother.

"If you can count a camel as family."

"Three is better than two," said Timoken.

And so they began the long, long journey across the desert. Sometimes they would come upon a group of nomads traveling with their goats. The strangers would eye the children with suspicion. What were they doing, all alone, on a camel decked out in finery? And then they would remember that the desert was full of tricks: phantom voices, wavering lights, and often a mirage of trees and water. And the nomads would begin to smile, believing the children must be a sign, sent from a star, to bring good luck.

One night, as the children lay in the shelter of an outcrop of rocks, Timoken gazed up into the sky and saw a narrow sliver of light slicing the velvet darkness. "The new moon," he exclaimed. "Remember what our mother said?"

Zobayda lit a candle and searched the bundle of possessions. When she found the bottle of Alixir, she poured one drop onto her finger and licked it. She put another onto Timoken's finger, and he did the same.

"And now Gabar," said Timoken.

Zobayda frowned. "Why?"

"Who knows how long the journey will take? We don't want our camel to grow old before we find a home."

"This liquid is precious," she argued. "It should not be wasted on a camel."

"Gabar is precious," Timoken insisted. Seizing the bottle, he took it over to the camel.

Gabar appeared to be dozing. He half-opened one large eye when Timoken approached.

"Gabar, I wish to put something on your tongue," said Timoken.

The camel was silent. His mouth remained closed.

"See, he doesn't want it," Zobayda called.

Timoken ignored her. "Gabar, open your mouth."

The camel shifted his leathery knees. "Why?"

"I want to put the smallest drop, the tiniest speck . . . a drib-let, a dot, if you like . . ."

"What is it?" asked Gabar.

"A liquid that will stop you from growing old," said Timoken.

"I shall never be old," said the camel. "There are old camels and young camels. I am young and will always be so."

Timoken scratched his head. It seemed that aging did not enter a camel's field of understanding. "Perhaps you could open your mouth, just for me?" said Timoken.

Without another word — or even a grunt — Gabar obediently opened his mouth.

Timoken stared at the huge teeth jutting out of the shadowy hole that was the camel's mouth. He tilted the bottle and let a drop fall on the camel's tongue, and then, because it was dark and his hand was unsteady, a second droplet slipped out.

The next day the camel seemed to have an extra spring in his step, but the Alixir appeared to have had no other effect on him.

Little by little their surroundings were changing. Almost without noticing it, they had left the barren desert and were traveling through a landscape dotted with clumps of grass and low, windblown shrubs.

As evening approached, Timoken saw a cluster of white build-ings on the horizon. Both children had the same thought. Could this be their new home? They were so tired. Their minds were bruised by the punishing sweep of the brown desert, their eyes sore from the relentless sun, and their limbs aching from days in the camel saddle. They thought of the fountains in the secret kingdom, the breeze from feathered fans, and their mother's gentle hands.

Full of hope, Timoken urged the camel toward the town.

Gabar gave a nervous grunt. "I do not know this place."

"Nor do we," said Timoken, "but we are eager to find out what sort of place it is. Perhaps it could be our new home."

It had once been a fine town, but the wall that had protected it had crumbled away. Great stones lay buried in the sand, and wind had ravaged the place. Doors had caved in, roofs had collapsed, and piles of sand lined the streets.

There were plenty of people about, however, and in the center of the town they came upon a market square filled with stalls. Goats, donkeys, and camels nosed at the earth for scraps. Many of the animals were pitifully thin, their flanks scarred by constant beatings.

"Bad place," Gabar snorted. "Let us go!"

Timoken thought of the pitiless desert. He longed to sleep beneath a roof, to speak to a kind family. But there was no friendship in the glances that were thrown at them. He could see only suspicion and hostility.

"There will be another place," Zobayda whispered, "a better place than this."

Timoken nodded. "Let us leave," he grunted to the camel.

Gabar needed no encouragement. With a toss of his head, he whirled around and made for a street leading out of the square.

A loud voice called out. The language was strange, the sound deep and burbling. Timoken could make no sense of it. Other voices followed, and a group of figures ran out and barred the camel's way. Timoken clutched the reins; he was beginning to understand that these were not men. They were creatures, green and sinewy.

"Viridees!" said Gabar, snorting with fury. He shook off one of the creatures that had grabbed his harness, and bolted past him. The creature fell, screaming. Others yelled their fury. Gabar raced down a narrow alley, while the crowd of viridees roared behind him. A wall loomed at the far end of the street.

"We're caught!" cried Zobayda. "There's only one way out. Timoken, we must fly!"

"Not without Gabar," Timoken said grimly.

Zobayda screamed, "Camels can't fly!"

"Who knows?" Timoken spoke through gritted teeth.

"He's too heavy. We must leave him. They'll kill us, Timoken. I can see it in their eyes."

"I will not leave our camel in this miserable place!" Timoken shouted. "But I will have to lighten his load." He took out his pearl-handled knife and slashed at the strings that held the heavy bag of treasure. It crashed to the ground, and some of the viridees gathered around it, tearing at the straps. Others, however, were still intent on catching the children.

"Wall!" bellowed Gabar. "No way out."

Timoken leaned over the camel's neck. In a quiet, firm voice, he said, "Jump, Gabar, and you will fly."

"Camels do not fly," Gabar snorted.

"Believe me, you can," said Timoken.

"Then I will believe!"

The camel's trust in him was unexpected. Timoken had hardly believed his own words. Now he must make them come true. But what an absurd idea this was. How could he carry a camel into the sky?

The wall was now only a few yards away. Timoken closed his eyes. With one hand, he held the reins tight against his chest. He could feel the wild thumping of his heart, and he trembled. He leaned down and, with his free hand, grabbed a tuft of the camel's shaggy hair. With his mind and with his soul, he leaped for the sky.

The pull of gravity was immense. It took his breath away. It dragged at his body and thundered in his scalp. *Up! Up!* He felt his lungs would burst and his body break apart. But just when he began to think that he had tested his power too far, the camel's jolting stride changed into an unfamiliar swaying motion. The saddle stopped sliding. Timoken opened his eyes. He could see nothing but sky.

Not a sound escaped from Gabar. He appeared to have stopped breathing. Zobayda seemed too surprised to speak. Every ounce of Timoken's strength had left him. He was content to sail through the sky in a stupefied silence.

The blistering sun dropped below the horizon; the sky became a dark velvet blue. A gentle warmth brushed Timoken's face, and a passing bird called out at the astonishing sight of a camel in the air.

CHAPTER 5
The Ring

A wonderful adventure had begun. For more than a hundred years, Timoken and Zobayda roamed through the cities of Northern Africa. With her enchanted fingers, Zobayda multiplied the jewels they had saved from the treasure chest, and so they never went hungry, nor did Gabar.

The camel was not always obedient, however. Sometimes he did not want to fly. It was undignified, he said, to fly in front of other camels. They were not impressed to see one of their number in the air. It was not a camel-like thing to do. This complicated life for the children. Very often, flying was their only means of escape.

Exploring was fun, but there was danger everywhere for two children traveling alone, two children who traded shells and precious gems for food and clothing. They were frequently set upon by bandits and chased by kidnappers, and they only narrowly avoided the knives that were hurled at them. And then there were the viridees, hiding behind trees, in wells and caves and other shadowy places. They would rush out at the children, long arms grabbing, tongues lashing.

And Timoken would cry, "Fly, Gabar, fly!" pulling on the reins and tugging the hair on the camel's neck.

Gabar would glance about him, making sure that no other camels were watching. If there was even one anywhere near him, he would snort, "Not yet!" And the children would have to wait, breathlessly, until the camel allowed himself to be lifted aloft.

Every night, Timoken and Zobayda slept beneath the moon spider's web. They called it the moon cloak and knew they were safe beneath its silken threads. If ever they were caught without it, Zobayda would use her enchanted fingers to escape. She could shrivel, burn, and tear, and if anyone grabbed Timoken or Gabar, she only had to point her fingers at the would-be captor and he would let go, screaming with fear and pain.

Not everyone was cruel. Kindness was often shown to the children. They would be given a meal for no reward and a safe bed in a house of great warmth and friendliness. And the orphaned children would begin to think of making a home in the city. But the very next day they could be chased and tormented, and they would have to forget their dream.

"We will never find a home in these heartless cities," Zobayda said one day. "I'm so tired of flying away, my heart throbbing and my breath caught in my throat."

Timoken looked at his sister, still only thirteen years old after more than a hundred years of traveling. He regarded his own small fingers and said, "If we had grown like ordinary people, they would leave us alone."

Zobayda shook her head. "Remember what our mother said. We mustn't start to grow until we find a real home." She spoke so sternly Timoken couldn't argue.

They decided to avoid the cities for a while, and traveled through the rough scrubland that bordered the desert. The nomad tribes had taught them how to bind their heads and faces with cloth to protect them from sandstorms, and they had learned how to survive the heat and discomfort. They often came within sight of a forest, but, although Gabar would go as far as the streams that trickled from the trees, he would go no farther. He was afraid of the darkness, the fleeting shadows, and the eerie sounds of birds and monkeys. Perhaps he sensed the strong presence of the viridees.

The viridees never lost track of Timoken and his sister. They tried every trick they knew to steal the moon cloak. They bribed merchants, beggars, and even beasts to destroy the children, but the moon cloak had a power of its own, and all their efforts failed.

Lord Degal had an idea. If the girl could be prevented from using her fingers, she could be captured. And for her safe return, surely the boy would hand over the web and the bottle.

"It is her ring," said Lord Degal. "That is what protects her. We must steal the ring."

He called for his best singer, a viridee whose voice could not be resisted. Lord Degal told the singer to practice the sweet tones of a bubbling stream.

Then, one achingly hot and tiring day, Timoken managed to urge the reluctant Gabar farther into the cool shade of a forest. The viridees were delighted. The singer could now lure Zobayda toward a stream. There she would dip her hands, attracted by a gleam beneath the water, something pretty — flowers like diamonds or pebbles like pearls. As soon as her fingers were underwater, a viridee could draw off the ring, rendering her fingers harmless.

And then we can catch her, they whispered with a chuckle.

After a night in the forest, the children were eating by their fire when Zobayda gave a little start, as though a mouse had run across her knees.

"What is it?" asked Timoken, licking his fingers.

"I felt something." Zobayda clutched her ringed finger. The ring seemed heavier today, and the little face looked anxious. Zobayda sensed that it was trying to warn her. "Timoken, you must never speak of your powers, never. No one must know that you can fly, that you can speak to animals and change the weather . . . no one."

"But some are bound to guess. They have seen us flying on Gabar."

"True," Zobayda murmured. Her dark eyes looked distant, and her next words were spoken as though she were receiving them from someone else. "You must not use your powers unless there is no other way."

In spite of the fire, Timoken felt suddenly chilled. His sister's tone was so solemn.

"But why?" he said.

Zobayda gave her brother a wide smile. "Don't worry, little brother. I know you will do your best to keep your secrets. Your place in the world is already foretold."

What did she mean? Timoken shivered with apprehension. He stared into the small flames, willing them to cheer him. "What do you mean?" he whispered to his sister.

"I hardly know myself." Zobayda stood up and brushed the creases from her robe. "It is just a sense I have. I'm going to fetch some fresh water. I can hear such a sparkling, rushing stream." She turned a full circle, gazing through the trees. "It's somewhere very near."

"Let me come," said Timoken.

"No. I can find it." She picked up their small clay jar and ran through the trees.

A little way off, Gabar had been standing in grumpy silence. Now he gave a loud grunt, and then another, and another.

"What's the matter?" called Timoken.

"Bad," said Gabar. "Worse and worse. Don't like forests."

All at once, Timoken agreed with him. "I'm sorry," he said. "We'll leave this forest when Zobayda gets back."

Zobayda followed the sound of the stream. It made an enchanting tinkle, almost like music. She had an overwhelming thirst now, and longed to feel the trickle of water over her tongue.

The stream, when she found it, was all she could have wished for. It bubbled and rushed over glistening pebbles, deep in one place, wide and gleaming in another. She ran beside it, farther and farther, drawn toward an even greater sound: the thunder of a waterfall. Before she reached the falls, she stopped at a shallow pool. She could see a bright sparkle under the swaying river-weeds, so bright it must be something precious. She knelt on a flat black rock beside the water and put out her hand. A sharp pain traveled up her arm. If she had looked at her ring she would have seen a grimace of fear on the small face, its mouth wide open, its eyes shut tight.

"No, no, no," came a tiny whisper.

Zobayda heard nothing but the pounding of the falls. Ignoring the pain, she dipped her hand in the water, reaching for that captivating sparkle. But as her fingers felt their way through the water, the weeds began to wrap themselves around her hand. They clasped her wrist, her arm. She put in her other hand to rescue the first, but that too was gripped by the dark weeds, and Zobayda cried out as the ring was slowly, very slowly, dragged from her finger.

As soon as the ring was gone, Zobayda's arms were released and she fell back on the rock. When she got to her feet and turned to run, she was certain that the trees behind her had moved closer. She stood, unsure, on the rock. The trees began to bend and twist, snakelike. They dipped and shivered and became tall green forms. The forms moved closer and closer. Zobayda could see the hint of a red eye, and then another. She saw arms, like vines, rippling beneath the shining leaves, and she guessed what those wicked forms wanted.

"You mean to exchange me for the moon cloak!" Her voice shook, but it carried, loud and fierce, above the noise of the falls. "And that you will never do."

The viridees stretched their sinewy green arms toward her, and Zobayda backed up to the very edge of the flat black rock. "The moon cloak belongs to my brother," she cried. "And it always will!" And turning swiftly, she jumped.

Burbling triumphantly, the viridees watched her black hair floating in a circle of silvery bubbles, as the current dragged her to the roaring falls. And then she was gone.

Timoken paced around the dead embers of the fire. The sun was rising; the forest was already steaming with damp heat. The sound of birds and beasts grew louder. Where was Zobayda? She had been gone far too long.

"I'm going to find my sister," Timoken told the camel. Draping the moon cloak around his shoulders, he set off.

Gabar would not be left on his own. He followed Timoken through the trees. The camel's feet moved awkwardly over the forest floor; he stumbled on creepers and leaves, and twigs kept entangling his head. He grunted unhappily.

Ignoring the camel's distress, Timoken bounded toward the sound of water. He found the stream and began to follow it. The stream became a river, and Timoken heard the roar of a waterfall. He halted and called his sister's name, but he found that his throat was choked with dread. Moving slowly now, he came to the flat black rock. He knew, somehow, that Zobayda had been standing there. He could almost see her.

Timoken walked to the edge of the rock. His hands were shaking, and the sound of his heart drummed in his ears. What had happened here? He knelt at the edge of the rock. Beneath his hands, the rock told its story. Zobayda's feet had been planted on its wet black surface. And then they had gone. They had leaped into the fast-flowing river. Why?

Timoken peered into the weeds that writhed under the surface of the water. Something shone there, on a narrow ledge that jutted from beneath the rock. Sweeping his hand across the ledge, Timoken touched a small object. When he brought it out, he found himself looking at Zobayda's ring. The forest-jinni's face was contorted with remorse.

"I could not stop them," came the whisper.

Tears of anger welled in Timoken's eyes. "Who?" he demanded.

A featherlight sound came from the ring. "Viridees."

That name again.

"Why?" roared Timoken. "Why her and not me?" He closed his fist around the ring and made to hurl it into the river.

"No-o-o-o-o!" screamed the ring.

Timoken gritted his teeth and growled, "Why should I keep you? You couldn't save my sister." He opened his fist, expecting the ring to drop into the torrent. But the ring clung to his finger and its voice carried, clear as a bell, over the roar of water.

"I tried to save her, Timoken. But they were too strong. I wouldn't let them take me, though. I belong to you, now."

"You're no use to me," cried Timoken, shaking his hand, trying to rid himself of the ring.

"You'll see! You'll see!" wailed the little voice.

There was a sudden rush of sound behind Timoken. It was as if every creature in the forest were echoing the words of the ring. *You'll see! You'll see! You'll see!*

"Keep me! Keep me!" cried the ring.

And a thousand chattering, screeching, howling voices chanted, *Keep the ring! Keep the ring!*

Timoken's hand dropped to his side. He turned and looked at the forest in astonishment. "Did you hear that?" he asked the camel.

"Keep the ring," Gabar advised.

Timoken muttered, "I suppose I will."

He slipped the ring on the middle finger of his left hand. An expression of weary relief appeared on the little face. Gently, it closed its eyes.

Timoken stepped off the black rock and leaned his head against Gabar's shaggy neck. "What shall we do without her?" he sobbed.

Gabar did not entirely understand human emotion, and yet Timoken's grief-stricken sounds echoed deep inside the camel and, to his surprise, he felt a tear trickling from one of his large eyes. Nevertheless, he had his own interests at heart. "We should leave the forest," he snorted.

"Not yet," sobbed Timoken. "Not yet." For, in the secret kingdom, those who grieved went into the forest and there they stayed until the grieving was over. That could be any time between one year and ten.

Wiping his eyes, Timoken began to stumble through the trees. Gabar followed obediently. They walked until nightfall, Timoken unable to stem the tears that streamed down his face. He could not rest. He could not eat or drink. Grief sat on his shoulders like a flat black rock, and he couldn't escape it.

They walked through the night. The cloud bats that Timoken had once found so entrancing, now seen through swollen eyes, appeared as insubstantial as floating dust. The calls of the owls that he had once listened to with such delight now sounded no more than a muttering of leaves.

They walked until dawn. As light and birdsong began to fill the forest, Timoken became aware that something was wrong. He looked over his shoulder.

Gabar was not there.

CHAPTER 6
The Hunter

"GABAR!" Timoken's desperate voice lifted through the trees, and anxious monkeys leaped along the branches.

"Help me!" Timoken called up to them. "Help me find him!"

His grief forgotten, Timoken was like a creature launched from a spring. Bounding and flying through the trees, he called to his camel, the only family he had left.

Birds and monkeys took up the call. "Gabar! Gabar! Gabar!"

The answering grunt that Timoken longed for didn't come. It wasn't until nightfall that a weary, reluctant sound drifted toward him.

The camel was sitting in a patch of moonlight. When Timoken approached, Gabar batted his long eyelashes, but gave no hint that he was pleased to see the boy.

"Gabar, are you ill?" Timoken sat beside the camel and patted his neck.

Gabar chewed on a thick leaf. He didn't like the flavor, but everything in the forest tasted bitter. "My head throbs," he said, "my stomach churns, and my feet hurt."

Timoken sighed. "I'm sorry, Gabar."

"Sorry?" queried the camel.

"I am sad for you," explained Timoken.

"No," said the camel. "You are sad for your sister who is gone. But you are not sad for me. If you were, you would leave the forest."

"I can't," moaned Timoken. "It is the custom of my people to grieve in the forest. I can't leave just yet. I am grieving for my sister."

"Custom?" snorted Gabar. He got to his feet. "It is my custom to walk on sand, and so I shall leave you and find the desert." He began to walk away.

"Gabar, no," wailed Timoken, running beside the camel. "Please stay with me."

"If I stay here, I shall die," Gabar snorted.

"You are my family," cried Timoken. "I thought I was yours."

"Good-bye, Family," said the camel.

Timoken realized that he had no choice. If he didn't want to be alone he would have to follow Gabar. All the camel's senses were leading him back to the world he knew. Timoken promised himself that he would grieve for his sister another time. "I will never forget you, Zobayda," he muttered. "But Gabar is all the family I have."

The forest was beginning to thin. The heat of the sun inten-
sified. Soon they would be out of the trees. The animal noises
were changing. Not so many monkeys here, not so many birds.
Even so, the silence, when it came, was very sudden.

Timoken was aware of a sound slicing through the air above
his head, so fast it could hardly be heard. There was a strangled
roar of pain and then a profound hush.

The forest held its breath, and the skin of Timoken's neck
prickled with fear. Caught in the silence of the trees, he could
hardly breathe. All at once, he was running. The camel trotted
after him.

They came to a clearing and Timoken scanned the undergrowth. Was it here? Was this where he was meant to come?
That muffled, desperate roar had led him here. Or was it fate?
A movement caught his eye, in the shadows behind the sunlit
trees.

Timoken gasped. The rotting branch resting against a tree
was, in fact, a creature. Tall and reed-thin, its green hair dangled
in vinelike strands over its slimy body. A quiver of arrows hung
from the belt around its waist, and its rootlike fingers rested on
the end of a large bow. A viridee.

Sounds reached Timoken at last. The forest had woken from
its trance. He could hear snarls and whimpers and the crunch of
bones. Behind the viridee hunter, a pack of hyenas was tearing at
the carcass of a small gazelle.

Timoken felt the viridee's gaze upon him. Its eyes were red, like embers without the black dot of a pupil, without a heart. Pitiless, they bored into his very bones.

Timoken took a step back and, as he did so, he glimpsed another body. A female leopard lying on her side. There was an arrow sticking out of her neck, the tip deeply embedded. The leopard's eyes were glazed. She was obviously dead.

Anger and disgust made Timoken's stomach lurch. The hunter had killed the leopard, and yet he was prepared to let hyenas eat the leopard's prey. One of the animals carried a piece of meat to the hunter, but the tall green figure did not take it. Still gazing at Timoken, he caressed the hyena's head.

This was no place for Timoken. The hyenas repelled him, and the rotting green figure gave off an overpowering scent of evil. The boy turned his back and began to run.

With the dreadful scene still burning in his mind, Timoken was blind to the creeper strung across his path. He tripped and fell, landing in a tangle of undergrowth. There was a weak hiss, and a tiny growl. Timoken turned his head and looked into the eyes of three small leopard cubs. They were huddled together behind a tangle of vines hanging from a fallen tree, only an arm's length from his face.

The cubs gave tiny defiant cries and, instinctively, Timoken put out a warning hand. "Hush!" He used a leopard's voice. "You are safe!"

The cubs stared at him with troubled eyes and then, one by one, approached and rubbed their heads against his cheeks. As

Timoken stroked their dappled fur, he was consumed by a rage that he had never known. He felt it almost before he knew the reason for it.

These small cubs would soon die. Without their mother, they were helpless. She had been carrying the dead gazelle when she was shot. And it was her prey that the hyenas were gorging on.

Timoken pulled the moon cloak from his shoulders and wrapped it around the cubs. They gazed at him, but did not attempt to shake off the web. Their wide gray eyes followed the boy as he stood and took out his pearl-handled knife.

"What are you doing, Family?" Gabar asked nervously.

"Shh!" warned Timoken. "I am going to get some meat."

"I hope not," grunted Gabar.

"Shh!" Rage filled Timoken's throat.

Gabar had never known the boy to use this kind of voice. Never. The sound puzzled him. Afraid of what would happen next, the camel fell silent. Motionless, he watched the boy creep soundlessly through the trees, back to the hideous scene he had just fled.

The viridee had already seen him. Red eyes marked the boy's movements as he stepped into the glade. Two of the hyenas looked up from their feast and snarled. Facing those long teeth, Timoken knew his little knife could not protect him. But he did not lower it, and he did not stop or back away. The hyenas were all looking at him now, their snarls and screams filling the air.

Timoken began to speak. He hardly knew where the words were coming from, but he was aware that he was using the voice of an animal. He spoke of the hyenas' children, of horrible pain, of the end of life.

The hyenas lowered their heads. Meat slid from their bloody jaws and their snarls turned to whimpers. Timoken stepped closer. Any fear he might have felt had been replaced by his unflinching will. All at once, to his astonishment, the whole pack turned their backs and ran, whining, into the trees.

But the hunter stayed where he was, red eyes flashing. With one fluid movement, his long fingers reached for an arrow.

For a fraction of a second Timoken was afraid. Could he grab the gazelle before the arrow reached him? As the hunter lifted his bow, the boy had his answer. Pointing his ringed finger at the treetops, he cried to the sky.

The answering crack of thunder startled the hunter, but it did not deter him. He fitted the arrow to his bow and drew it back. The second crack of thunder came with a blinding flash. A shaft of lightning struck the tree beside the viridee. Before he could move, the tree crashed to the ground, crushing the viridee beneath its flaming branches.

Fire snaked along the fallen tree and crackled in the under-growth. Seizing the gazelle carcass, Timoken carried it through the forest, while the fire snapped and hissed behind him. He heaved the length of meat toward the cubs' hiding place and laid it before them. Three small heads appeared between the hanging creepers. Cautiously, the cubs crept from beneath the moon cloak and sniffed the meat. Excited by the smell, they began to eat: tearing, chewing, and whimpering with hunger and delight.

"Look! Look, Gabar," Timoken said joyfully. "I got the meat. I've fed them, and they will live!"

Gabar had taken several paces away from the scene. What he saw worried him. He had never liked the smell of raw meat, and it unsettled him to see these three dangerous creatures tearing at it.

"Aren't you proud of me, Gabar?" Timoken asked. "I wish you had seen those hyenas slink away."

"There is a fire," the camel grunted. "Soon we will all be burned to death."

Timoken leaped up with a gasp. "I forgot!" Seizing the moon cloak, he whirled it in an arc above his head, again and again. His calls rose through the forest, and the rain answered him. It poured through the leaves and splashed against the trees, extinguishing the fire in seconds.

Timoken wrapped the moon cloak around his wet shoulders and laughed with pleasure. The rain stopped, but the cubs, now wet through, continued to eat. Even when their bellies were full they went on gnawing, their fear of hunger driving them on. When their sleepy eyes began to close, Timoken pushed the carcass into the hollow beneath the tree, and the cubs crawled in after it. In a few minutes they were fast asleep. Timoken covered them with the moon cloak and went in search of Gabar, who had wandered off.

He found the camel drinking from a stream. Timoken untied the bag of food hanging from the saddle, and pulled out some millet cakes.

Gabar turned his head and looked at the boy. "You will have to kill," the camel said. "Those cubs will grow. They'll eat you and me, unless you feed them."

"I'll steal more carcasses," said Timoken. "I'm not afraid of hyenas."

"Hmf!" The camel chewed a long twig. "It won't be enough. And what about milk?"

"Milk?" Timoken looked at Gabar. "Do you mean . . . ?"

"Don't look at me," said Gabar. "I shall never be a mother."

"But those cubs might need someone's mother, that's what you're saying. They might need milk as well as food."

The camel blinked in agreement.

"I will find a goat," Timoken said blithely. "There's bound to be a goat somewhere."

Unconvinced, Gabar pursed his rubbery lips.

While the cubs slept, Timoken lay on the fallen tree above them. In more than a hundred years of traveling he had never saved a life. The experience had changed him. If he had lived like an ordinary mortal, he would be dead by now. And so, it followed, would the cubs. Fate had brought them together, and now he felt bound to the small creatures he had saved. "Forever," he murmured to himself.

Timoken closed his eyes and began to devise a way to carry the cubs. Nomads had given him a small bag for water, and now the big goatskin bag hung empty from the saddle. The cubs could be carried in it.

Timoken chewed a millet cake and then drifted off to sleep. He woke up to find Gabar's nose in his face.

"Family," said the camel, "you have forgotten something."

"What?" Timoken answered drowsily.

"You never sleep without a cover. The viridees will come back. The forest is not safe."

Timoken smiled. "You are right. But first, the cubs." He lifted the curtain of creepers and looked into the dark hollow where they slept.

The moon cloak now covered the cubs completely. It had wrapped itself around them, and billowed gently with their heart-beats. The shining threads seemed to embrace the cubs, as though the web was claiming them for its own. One cub lay on his back; the others were curled on each side of him, their heads pressed against his. Seen through the veil of spider silk, the markings on their fur appeared like a scattering of stars.

Timoken drew in his breath and sat back.

"What?" asked Gabar.

"They have become . . ." Timoken didn't know how to describe what he saw to the camel.

Gabar waited patiently for the rest of Timoken's answer.

"Enchanted," said Timoken, hoping that the camel would understand.

He did.

CHAPTER 7
Sun Cat, Flame Chin, and Star

There were five of them now. "A family of five," Timoken liked to say. But the camel did not agree. He was not entirely comfortable when the leopards were close.

They were traveling through grassland, country that was neither forest nor desert. Gabar was happy on the dry, flat earth. There were water holes and streams and sometimes a low, tasty tree. And the camel knew that Timoken could keep dangerous animals away with the loud sounds he made, in languages that Gabar couldn't begin to understand.

The cubs enjoyed riding in the big goatskin bag. Sometimes, they would peek above the rim and watch the world go by. But as soon as they caught the scent of a big cat, they would duck down into the bag.

Whenever they passed a group of nomads, Timoken would exchange a fistful of shells for a bag of goat's milk.

The first time the cubs tasted goat's milk, they pronounced it very good.

"As good as your mother's milk?" Timoken asked the cubs.

"No," said the biggest cub. Timoken called him Sun Cat. His coat was darker than his brothers', the markings larger and closer, and in certain lights his spots took on a shade of sunset red. One of his brothers had a hint of orange beneath his chin, like a small flame. Timoken named him Flame Chin. The smallest of the three had a coat as pale as a star. He was always the last to approach Timoken, but it was this cub that he loved best. He called him Star.

Every night, Timoken slept under the moon cloak with the cubs snoring beside him. In the morning, he would tie the goatskin bag to Gabar's saddle and lift the cubs into it. But one morning they struggled when Timoken lifted them, and begged to be set free.

"We will follow," said Sun Cat.

"We will watch," said Flame Chin.

"We will listen," said Star.

Reluctantly, Timoken climbed onto the camel's back and left the cubs to run beside them. After a while they fell behind, and when Timoken looked back, they had vanished. He didn't know what to do.

"Stop, Gabar," he commanded, pulling on the reins. "The cubs are lost."

"No," grunted the camel. "You cannot see them. They are not lost."

"How do you know?" Timoken demanded. "Can you smell them, hear them, sense them?"

Gabar gave a grunt that was more like a sigh of impatience. "Leopards are not seen," he said. "They must NOT be seen. You should be proud that they have learned this so quickly."

"Oh!" Timoken was always being surprised by the camel's vast knowledge. "I am proud," he said. "Very proud."

Timoken did not see the cubs again all day. But that night, while he lay sleepless with anxiety beneath the moon cloak, three shadowy forms crept out of the long grass and crawled in beside him.

They continued in this way for several days, but one night the cubs did not return. The moon was, once again, a thin splinter in the sky, but Timoken forgot the Alixir. The new moon had almost disappeared when Gabar said, "Family, do you want to grow old?"

"The Alixir!" Timoken found the bird-shaped bottle. He gave the camel a single dose, and then poured a drop for himself.

Three weeks later, the cubs reappeared.

Timoken and Gabar had reached a range of tall, seemingly impassable mountains. For several days they had been traveling north across a stretch of inhospitable, stony ground. The nights were growing colder. Darkness was falling fast and Timoken decided to light a fire. Gabar settled himself close to the flames and began to doze. Timoken leaned against the camel and closed his eyes. How long, he wondered, and how far would he have to roam before he found a home? Gabar was very dear to him, but he sometimes longed for the companionship of another human being. He thought of his sister and tears welled in his eyes. Timoken pressed his fists against his lids. He was more than a hundred years old, so he should not cry.

A voice, close to his ear, whispered, "North."

Timoken looked at the ring on the middle finger of his left hand. The small silver face wore a frown. "North," it urged again.

"I have come North," Timoken said irritably.

"Farther," the voice implored. "Now."

There was a sudden, loud rumble from the camel: a nervous warning sound. Timoken jumped up and searched the rocky scrubland before him. Nothing moved, but it was dark and he could not see what lay beyond the firelight. The grasses beside him rustled and a dreadful stench came out of them. Timoken froze. He knew that smell. He leaped for the moon cloak, lying behind him, but he was too late.

Long, sinewy arms grabbed the web and tossed it away. Timoken could see them now: three tall figures, twisting and bending, one to his left, another on his right, and the third a few feet in front of him, waving the moon cloak like a banner.

"I have it," one of the viridees shrieked, and his laughter filled the air like the tuneless scream of a hungry hyena.

The web was not easy for him to hold. It fought back, stinging his rootlike fingers and burning his boneless arms. But he would not give it up. As Timoken reached for the web, the laughing viridee tossed it to another. They raced away from Timoken, shrieking and gurgling, as they threw the web from one to another.

Timoken's anger swept every thought from his mind. Forgetting the storms he might bring, or the swift flight he could make, he stumbled over the rocky ground while the viridees sped ahead. Blind with rage, Timoken was not aware of the rock that lay in his path until he ran full pelt into it and crashed to the stony ground.

Beating the stones with his fists, Timoken cried, "No! No! No!"

For a moment he did not notice the change of tone in the viridees' voices, and then, suddenly, he realized that their gleeful cries had become wild with fear.

Staggering to his feet, Timoken saw three dark forms leap upon the viridees. Their cries crescendoed to deafening shrieks and then died to a single moan, until the only sounds were the deep growls of the three leopards as they sniffed their victims' lifeless bodies.

As Timoken cautiously approached, Sun Cat carried the moon cloak over to him and laid it at his feet. The other cubs joined him and they stood, all three, before the boy. In a sudden blaze from the fire, Timoken could see that, in three weeks, the cubs had grown. Their shoulders were wide and strong, their tails thick and heavy, and the hair on their big feet hinted at powerful claws.

"Thank you, my friends," said Timoken. He lifted the moon cloak and threw it around his shoulders.

"You must go," said Sun Cat.

"North," said Flame Chin.

"Now," said Star.

"Now? But my enemies are dead. Can we not sleep, Gabar and I? We are so weary."

"No time," said Sun Cat.

"Fly," said Flame Chin.

"Over the mountain," said Star.

"But —"

"NOW!" said all three. "It is not safe here."

The leopards' voices were so grave, Timoken ran to his camel, crying, "We must go, Gabar. Now. At once."

"Now?" grumbled the camel, in disbelief.

The bags were still all in place, and after quickly dousing the fire, Timoken climbed into the saddle. "Up, Gabar, up!" he cried.

"Up?" Gabar slowly got to his feet.

"We must fly."

"Where?"

"Over the mountain."

"Oh, no," the camel moaned.

"Fly!" yelled Timoken, and he pulled on the camel's shaggy hair, willing him up the steep side of the mountain.

They passed jagged ledges and rough, crumbling stones, where no man or beast had ever walked, and there was nowhere to rest. Up, up, and up. The camel bellowed in fear and pain, gasping for air. Timoken looked for sky above the mountain, but saw only the rugged wall of rock, rising into nowhere.

"Rest!" grunted the camel. "Family, I beg."

"There is nowhere to rest," croaked Timoken, the cold air filling his lungs. "Up, Gabar, up!"

For a moment Gabar hung in the air, unable to rise any farther, and Timoken, feeling the dead weight of the camel, cried with the pain in his arms and chest. "We must fly up," he groaned. "We must, Gabar." He gave an almighty tug, and this time the camel came with him, farther and farther into the white drifts of clouds and out again into a radiant, starlit sky.

They flew a little way beyond the mountain peaks, and then slowly descended into another country entirely. From below came the distant murmur of waves breaking on a shore.

CHAPTER 8
The House of Bones

They landed in darkness on a small island in the center of a vast lake. Timoken led Gabar over a beach of rattling shells into the shelter of some trees. There, exhausted by their flight, they both fell fast asleep.

When he woke up, Timoken ran on to the beach. The shells looked valuable and he put some in his bag before venturing farther.

How could he know that, for hundreds of years, the viridees had lured travelers and fishermen to this solitary island? There they would be robbed of all they possessed and left to die. When the island viridees saw Timoken and the camel flying toward them, they could not believe their luck. How pleased Lord Degal would be when they presented him with the web of the last moon spider. For, this time, they had a trap that Timoken would never escape.

Timoken left the beach and wandered back into the trees. The ground was covered in a thick blanket of flowers and broad-leaved shrubs. The island appeared to be deserted; he couldn't even hear a bird. Timoken decided to explore. Leaving Gabar to rest, he picked his way through the undergrowth.

A building appeared through the trees and Timoken made his way toward it. The building was circular, with a white domed roof, and walls veined with gold that shimmered in the sunlight. The pillars on either side of the arched entrance were decorated with strange symbols. Timoken could make no sense of them.

What was inside the building? Who had built it? Timoken hesitated. Something told him not to go any farther, but his curiosity got the better of him. He mounted the three marble steps up to the entrance and went in.

He was immediately engulfed by an overwhelming darkness. There was not the tiniest scrap of light anywhere, even though the sun had been shining through the open doorway. Timoken turned around. He could see nothing. The doorway had gone. He walked forward and touched a cold stone wall. Feeling his way along the wall, he was sure that, sooner or later, he would find a door frame, a crack in the wall — anything to indicate an opening. He began to stumble on twigs or pebbles underfoot. Bending to find out what could be lying on the floor, his hand gripped a long, smooth object with a rounded, knobbly end. Timoken dropped it and felt for another. There were similar objects, like twigs, jagged and bony.

It was when he touched the skull that Timoken knew, beyond any doubt, that the crackling, crunching things beneath his feet were the bones of a human body. And there was definitely more than one. The floor was littered with bones.

Timoken opened his mouth and screamed. But there was only Gabar to hear him. And what could a camel do? Timoken tried to think of a power that could help him. He could fly, he could bring a storm, he could speak to any animal in the world, but how could he escape from this terrible house of bones? He did not even have the moon cloak to protect him.

But he had the ring. He ran his fingers over it. A frail light appeared on his ringed finger, and the forest-jinni's tiny face looked out at him.

"What can I do?" begged Timoken. "Can you help me?"

"Their power is very strong here," the forest-jinni said sorrowfully.

"The viridees?"

"Indeed."

"You said you would help me," cried Timoken, "but you cannot."

"They drain me." The tiny voice was not much more than a breath of air. "They are too strong." The ring's light began to fade.

"Fight them, forest-jinni. I beg you. Be strong."

The jinni's eyes were closing, but suddenly they blinked open. "Call the leopards," he whispered.

"I can't!" wailed Timoken. "They won't hear me. And how can they reach me?"

"The web has made them different from other creatures: marvelous, amazing, immortal. . . ." The weak thread of the tiny voice ran out. The light faded and the silence that followed was so thick and so absolute it forced Timoken to his knees. He swept his hands over the rubble of bones, and a huge anger burned inside him. How many people had the viridees tricked and killed in this dreadful place? He refused to be one of them.

He remembered the language of the leopards and a roar rose into his throat. Such a huge roar, it made him shake. It burst out of his mouth and filled the darkness.

Again and again, the voice of a furious leopard echoed up to the roof and bounced off the walls. Gabar heard the sound and stumbled to his feet. He was already worried. Timoken had been gone too long. That sound was like no other. It was a leopard's roar, but Gabar knew Timoken's voice by now.

The big camel began to plod through the trees toward the sound of the leopard. A black cloud rolled across the sky and the sunlight was gone, leaving the island in gloomy shadow. When Gabar reached the building it was no longer beautiful. It was gray and unwelcoming. He could see an open doorway, and yet the noise that Timoken was making was that of a trapped animal. Why could he not get out?

Gabar thought, *A spell!* No sooner was the thought inside his head than the palm leaves above, and the plants all about him, began to whisper and murmur and chuckle and snarl.

"Family!" bellowed the terrified camel. "Viridees!"

Timoken heard the camel's desperate call, but he couldn't help him. So he gave another roar; a roar so deep and dangerous the wicked creatures that were even now stealing toward the camel hesitated for a moment before continuing on their greedy way.

Gabar wheeled around to see a crowd of thin green creatures creeping toward him. Their wet hair dangled, their red eyes flashed, and their long arms swung like slimy vines.

"Camel," said one. "Let us take your heavy burdens."

Gabar raised his head and bellowed. But rootlike fingers were now reaching for the bag that contained the moon cloak. Twisting his neck, Gabar bit, crunching the slimy arm between his big teeth. Then he kicked and howled, turned and turned, churning the earth with his furious feet.

Inside the house of bones, Timoken heard his camel bellowing. Angry and helpless, he slid to the floor and crouched among the piles of bones. He closed his eyes and growled in sympathy with his poor camel.

A thin light crept through his eyelids. The light grew stronger. Timoken opened his eyes and saw a flame burning outside a wall. He touched the wall, but felt only hard stone. He was baffled.

The flame outside began to circle the building, and Timoken had the impression that he was surrounded by a ring of fire. And now he could hear it, crackling and hissing. "Gabar!" he cried. "What's happening?"

He was answered by the roar of a leopard. Three roars. Three leopards.

The circle of fire grew brighter. Timoken could feel the heat of it through the walls. He could smell the scorched stones. The walls began to crumble; stones tumbled out and rolled down the steps. Through the gaps, Timoken could see trees and Gabar, his big eyes wide with amazement. But the leopards had no shape at all. They were flashes of fire, joined in a ring by tails of flame.

Timoken pushed and kicked the walls until he had made a gap wide enough to squeeze through. The stones were hot, but he managed to slip past them without burning his clothes. As soon as he was through, the building behind him came crashing to the ground. Timoken leaped away from the flying rubble and burst through the fiery circle without feeling a thing.

The flames began to evaporate into the air. And there were the leopards. They stood shoulder to shoulder: Sun Cat, Flame Chin, and Star.

"You saved my life," purred Timoken.

"Our lives are yours," the big cats purred in return.

Sun Cat said, "Go now!"

"This place is bad," said Flame Chin.

"Be safe," said Star.

"But you . . . how will you . . . ?"

"Nothing can hurt us," said Sun Cat.

"We are faster than wind," said Flame Chin.

"We will always be with you," said Star.

"So leave this place now!" The three roars came all at once, and there was no mistaking the urgency in their voices.

Gabar had already crouched for Timoken to mount.

The boy looked all about him, into the trees and lush green undergrowth. But there was no sign of the viridees. The leopards had frightened them away — for now. The dark cloud had folded back from the sun, and the house of bones was now a mound of rubble.

Timoken climbed into the saddle, and Gabar lifted himself from his knees.

"I'm sorry, Gabar," Timoken began, "but —"

"I know. We must fly again," said Gabar. "I am happy about it."

Timoken could not stifle his laugh. Gabar often lightened his mood in the most difficult situations.

"So, let's fly!" Timoken grabbed Gabar's shaggy hair and up they went, with no effort at all.

When Timoken looked down, the leopards had vanished, but their roars followed him across the gleaming stretch of water. "Be safe, Small King! Be wise! Be well!"

Soon Timoken could see a distant green line emerging on the horizon of the great blue lake. As they drew nearer, he was relieved to see not a mountain range, but lush green trees and square, flat-roofed houses.

They landed on a sandy beach, where fishing boats rocked beside a wooden jetty. Two fishermen were mending their nets at the water's edge, and a boy was balancing a basket of fish on his head as he made his way from the jetty to the trees.

No one appeared to have noticed the camel's unusual arrival.

The fishermen, intent on their nets, paid no attention to the strangers. They did not even turn their heads as Timoken led Gabar up to the trees.

It was a quiet place. The market was hardly busy. Timoken exchanged a handful of shells for some fruit and nuts. No one seemed surprised to see a boy alone with a camel. Perhaps they thought he was the servant of a rich master. He had covered his head with the striped hood of his robe, hiding the thin gold crown.

Will this be home? Timoken wondered. No, something was urging him on. He looked at the ring. It had lost its brilliance and the small face seemed asleep. Timoken wondered if the viridees had been too powerful for the little creature. Was he dead?

That evening, as he sat in a pine grove with Gabar munching nuts at his back, Timoken reached for his bag and took out a pearl. He let it roll around his palm for a minute, and then he attempted to multiply it, just as Zobayda had done. If the forest-jinni had lost his spirit, then the spell might not work. Timoken murmured simple words as he ran his finger over the pearl. "Let there be two, let there be three and four."

The pearl rocked to and fro, and then, suddenly, there were two. Then three. Then four. Timoken sensed that the forest-jinni had not taken part in the spell, but that he, Timoken, had multiplied the pearl without the help of the ring.

He slipped the ring off his finger, cupped the pearls in his hands, and held them against his cheek. "Five, six, seven, eight," he whispered. "Nine, ten, eleven, twelve." He continued count-ing to twenty. He could feel his hands filling up, the pearls pressing into his fingers. When he opened his hands, a stream of pearls fell into his lap.

"I can do it," Timoken breathed. "I can do it, all by myself."

A muffled sigh came from the ring. "You still need me." The forest-jinni's voice sounded desperate.

"Of course I do." Timoken picked up the ring and pushed it onto his finger. Multiplying the pearls made him feel powerful, more like the guardian of the ring, rather than the other way around.

Full of hope, he decided to continue his journey by starlight. He had already learned to use the constellations as a guide. Gabar did not object, and so they struck north. There was not even a dog awake to see the camel tread quietly through the vil-lage and out onto the sandy road that led—who knew where?

In the morning they reached another village, and the next day another. And so it went on until they got to the sea. Gradually, they made their way into a different sort of country. They passed the ruins of ancient palaces and temples. They saw pyramids and statues half hidden in the sand. And whenever he had a chance, Timoken would take out his pearl-handled knife and find a place where he could sketch his journey. He drew his pictures in cata-combs and caves, on the floors of abandoned temples, on castle ramparts and the walls of monastery gardens. Very often Charlie, the boy from the cave wall, would arrive, stealing in from the future while Timoken was drawing.

"I've found you!" Timoken's descendant would mutter into his ear. And Timoken would laugh with delight, and they would talk and talk, the words bubbling out of Timoken like a foun-tain, while Gabar watched them with a look of disapproval on his proud camel's face.

One day, when Timoken and Charlie were sitting together in the ruins of a Roman villa, Timoken said, "I have told you about my life as it has been for the past hundred and more years, but perhaps you know my future, Charlie. Can you tell me when I will die?"

The boy beside him frowned. "No," he said, "but my friend, Gabriel, has the cloak that you wore." He touched the moon cloak that rested on Timoken's shoulders. "It is red velvet, not like this moon cloak."

"Red, you say." Timoken smiled. "What kind of red?"

"Like a sunset."

When Charlie had gone, Timoken patted his camel's neck and said, "Don't look so disapproving, Gabar. I cannot help talk-ing so much with Charlie. I miss the company of other children, other beings like me."

The camel grunted, "Me, too!"

Timoken felt guilty. He knew that Gabar must miss the com-pany of other camels. But what could be done about it? If he found a companion for Gabar, how could he make it fly? He and Gabar were bound to each other, by time and events, and probably love.

They had slowly been traveling into a cold climate. Winter came, and for the first time in his life, Timoken saw snow falling. He knew what it was because he had seen it on the mountain peaks, but to sit on a camel's back while thick white flakes drifted softly about him was magical.

They traveled north, and every day seemed colder than the last. Timoken stopped to exchange some silk for a thick woolen blanket to cover Gabar's back, and for himself, a sheepskin cape and a fur hat. Soon they found themselves in a rocky, barren land where the north wind blew constantly. They spent the winter in a cave, only occasionally venturing out to exchange shells and beads for food. The leopards paid them a visit. When they were sure that all was well with Timoken, they vanished into the chilly gray landscape, promising always to listen for Timoken's call.

Spring came, and the boy and the camel moved on. Sometimes they would stay on the edge of the same village for almost a year, and sometimes they moved on, swiftly. They flew over a sea that Gabar thought would never end. They soared over mountains so high that the camel's hair froze into rigid tufts of ice, and Timoken thought his cold nose would drop off. But still the ring urged them on. "Not safe, yet," it would whisper.

*   *   *

Fifty more years passed, and Timoken decided he could go no farther. "We have come so far north," he complained to the ring. "Surely the viridees cannot reach us now."

The eyes in the tiny face blinked. "There is something new," he said, and a note of apology crept into his voice. "They have extended their grasp."

"I don't understand," said Timoken.

"I think . . . I sense . . . that one is human."

"If this person is human, then he, or she, is not a viridee."

"But he is . . . and yet . . . in most respects, he looks like a human."

"Where is this human viridee? Am I about to meet him?"

"How can I tell?" the forest-jinni said regretfully. "Forgive?"

"Of course I forgive you. But what am I to do?" Timoken clenched his fists in frustration. "Am I never to feel safe in the company of humans? Never to have a friend?" He twisted the ring, as though it were all the fault of the forest-jinni. "How will I know this . . . this person if I meet him? Will there be a sign? Will his true nature show in his face?"

"You will know," said the ring.

CHAPTER 9
The Girl in the Cage

In his two hundred and forty-fifth year, Degal, lord of the viridees, decided to travel north. He had outlived all his wives and now he wanted another. But this time she had to be human. Lord Degal wanted a son who could survive the biting chill of the north wind, who could walk in snow, and live quite happily in freezing temperatures. A human mother could give her son these strengths; then the boy could take the power inherited from his father into realms where no viridee had ever ventured.

Lord Degal had heard of a certain Count Roken of Pomerishi, who had fifteen daughters. Naturally, the count wanted to find a husband for all of his daughters. He had managed to marry off eight of them, but there were seven left. It was proving very expensive to feed and clothe these seven girls; they were fussier and more bad tempered than their married sisters. It was rumored that the count was so desperate to find husbands for his unmarried daughters that he was prepared to overlook any unpleasant features the husband-to-be might have, as long as the man had a horse.

Count Roken lived in the mountains of northern Europe, a place where, even in summer, a snowstorm could blow up. Lord Degal braced himself. His scouts found three strong horses and, together with two soldiers, Lord Degal rode out of the forest. In his saddlebag he carried enough gold to buy the fur coats, hats, and boots that they would need to survive the cold northern climate.

By the time the viridees reached Count Roken's castle their greenish skin had become quite blue, and one of the soldiers had lost a rootlike finger to frostbite.

Once inside the great hall, the three viridees began to lose their blue looks and became their usual shade of green. Count Roken decided to ignore this peculiarity. Dressed in his forest-green robes, Lord Degal looked very impressive. There were no wrinkles on his damp, greenish skin and, apart from a few strands of white, his hair was still the color of pond weed. The count was pleased to hear that his visitor was looking for a wife. He called for his daughters and Lord Degal watched keenly as, one by one, they entered the hall. As soon as he saw Adeliza, he knew that she was the one for him.

Adeliza was the count's most beautiful daughter. She was also the most heartless. She had brown-gold hair, cold green eyes, and a Cupid's bow mouth. But ten would-be husbands had turned her down. Her voice was so chilly, her gaze so cold, that young men ran from her like frightened mice. Not so Lord Degal. He recognized a kindred spirit.

For her part, Adeliza was fascinated by Lord Degal's long, boneless arms. She found his greenish skin and flickering red eyes strangely attractive, and when she heard of the black marble throne inset with emeralds, she could hardly wait to be married.

The wedding took place the following morning, and a day later, the happy couple was on their way back to Africa.

The African forest was hotter than Adeliza expected, but she did not complain. She enjoyed wearing priceless jewels and sparkling robes, and she delighted in having a thousand servants at her beck and call.

Lord Degal was pleased with his new wife, and when their son was born, he could tell, almost at once, that the boy would be everything he had wished for. They named him Harken, after Adeliza's grandfather.

The baby grew into a fine young man. He was handsome, ruthless, and cunning, and his sorcery was impressive. A glance from his olive green eyes could freeze you in a second. He could turn into a serpent, he could create monsters, and he had a natural talent for poisoning.

When Harken was thirteen, Lord Degal sent him north. "I want you to find an African boy who rides a flying camel," said the lord of the viridees. "This boy has something priceless, something that could make you very powerful."

"I am powerful," Harken replied carelessly. "And camels do not fly."

"This one does," said his father. "And you are not as powerful as the African."

Harken pricked up his ears. "Oh? How so?"

"The boy has the web of the last moon spider. It was dipped in dew held in rare flowers, and washed with the tears of creatures that will never be seen again. It can protect the wearer from any attack, any weapon in the world."

"But not from me," Harken remarked, with a haughty lift of his right eyebrow.

His father was becoming impatient. "How do you know?"

Harken shrugged.

"You had better go and find out."

Harken groaned. "Where is this boy and his flying camel?"

"My scouts tell me that he is heading for the mountains beyond the two seas." Lord Degal showed his son a map drawn on the dried skin of a warthog. "And there is something else," he added. "We believe that the boy is still in possession of a bird-shaped bottle. We do not know what it contains, but it might be a liquid that can help one to live forever, for the boy has not aged in two hundred years."

Harken's curiosity was aroused. Accompanied by four viridee soldiers, he left the forest and journeyed north, in search of a boy on a flying camel. Harken was good at finding things. He did not think it would take him long to track down the moon spider's web and the bird-shaped bottle.

In a few weeks, Harken's search had led him very close to the area where Timoken was traveling. But a wide valley still lay between them, and in that valley was a group of children who would dramatically affect the course of Timoken's life.

Inside a covered wagon, pulled by a weary horse, sat eleven kidnapped children. The wagon rocked and jolted its way across the valley, driven by a man dressed in the hooded brown robe of a monk. But he was not what his clothes might suggest. On the contrary, he was a villain — a kidnapper. His five companions, all dressed as he was, rode behind the wagon. Their spare horse was tied to the side.

The eleven children sat tied to one another by their wrists. Their mouths were bound with rags and their ankles roped together so tightly that their skin was grazed and sore. They had all been kidnapped.

Four British boys sat on one side of the wagon, their legs stretched between the legs of the seven French children opposite — four boys and three girls.

At the back of the wagon, beside one of the Britons, there was a cage, and in the cage there was another girl. She wore a long sky-blue dress and a brown fur-lined cape. Her blonde hair, braided with blue ribbons, reached to her waist. She sat with her legs curled to one side; her hands were bound, but her mouth and legs were free. The kidnappers obviously thought her skin too precious to mark with ropes or rags. She was, in fact, a daughter of the most famous soldier in Castile, though her present captors did not know this.

The wagon suddenly jolted to a halt, sending its occupants rolling against one another. They struggled upright and waited for something to happen. Were they to be rescued, or tortured?

Silhouetted against the moonlit sky, the broad outlines of two men appeared at the open end of the wagon. The men climbed up and began to remove the gags from around the children's mouths. As they walked between the rows of children, they roughly kicked and pushed their legs. One of the French girls began to whimper, and the boy next to her whispered, "Shh, Marie!" The other children were silent. They knew that if they cried out they would get no supper.

Pieces of black bread were handed out. At first the children had found it difficult to eat, tied to one another by their wrists. But they had learned always to use their right hands, leaving their left to be tugged up to their neighbor's mouth. They had to take care not to spill the water, passing the jug from one to the other without tipping it up too far.

When he reached the back of the wagon, one of the men opened the cage door and put a jug of water onto the floor. He placed a hunk of bread and cheese beside it.

The two men left the children and a few moments later the crackle of a fire could be heard. The kidnappers began to murmur to one another. One said, "In two days she will be off our hands." Another voice muttered, "What price did you ask?" The reply could not be heard. Soon the tantalizing smell of roast meat drifted into the wagon.

One of the Britons clutched his stomach and rolled his eyes. He was thirteen and almost the height of a man. His father was an archer, and he was fast becoming one himself before he was kidnapped. He was broad and strong and always hungry.

The copper-haired boy beside the cage said, "Do not make us laugh, Mabon. They will punish us!"

"The smell of meat is punishment enough," said Mabon.

Little Marie began to giggle. Henri, her neighbor, choked on his bread and soon they were all shaking with silent laughter.

The copper-haired boy glanced at the cage beside him, wondering if the girl was smiling. She had only been with them for a day, and so far she had not smiled once, even when he tried to tell her his name.

The girl stared at him and, once again, he pointed to his chest, saying, "Edern!"

The girl laid a hand against her own chest and said, "Beri!"

Everyone looked at the cage. It was the first time they had heard the girl speak. Was she British or French?

First Edern, then Henri, asked the girl where she came from. She would not reply to either of them.

Henri shrugged and said, "*Mysterieuse!*"

Gereint, the smallest Briton, began to sing, very softly. He had a beautiful voice. He sang in Latin, a language his singing master had taught him. It was like magic. The girl gave a beautiful smile and clung to the bars of her cage. A stream of words poured from her, but they were neither French nor English.

"Perhaps she is a Roman," said Mabon, when the girl sat back, still smiling at Gereint.

"The Romans are all dead," said the boy beside him. His name was Peredur. With his narrow face and long, sharp teeth, he looked like a golden-haired wolf.

While they continued to argue and chatter, Beri's thoughts were far away. Gereint's song had reminded her of the cathedral in Toledo. The last time she had entered the cathedral, it was to see her cousin married. Beri did not want to get married. Not ever. She had always wanted more from life. She had wanted adventure, excitement. Only her father knew that she was already an accomplished sword fighter. Their lessons had been held in secret. .

"If only I had a sword," she murmured to herself in Castilian.

"QUIET!" One of the kidnappers appeared. He was the cruelest of the six. His face was scarred and his nose flattened by years of fighting.

Mabon, who was nearest to the man, asked, "Please, sir, where are you taking us?"

The man stared hard at him. "How many times have you asked? I told you. You will know when you get there."

"Give us a clue," said Peredur bravely.

The man gave an ugly smile. "All right. You asked for it. You are going East, to a place where pale-skinned, golden-haired children like you fetch a very good price."

"Price?" Edern swallowed nervously.

"Slaves!" The man's crooked smile grew wider. "That is what you will be. And just so you know: There is not a house for miles, so you might as well save your voices."

When the kidnapper had gone a grave silence fell over the children. The French had not understood the man's words, but the Britons' desperate faces told them that things were not good.

As the wagon began to move again, Edern whispered to Peredur, "I am going to escape. I am the fastest runner, so I stand a chance. Will you use your teeth to help me, Perry?"

Peredur grimaced, showing his wolflike teeth. He lifted his hand and Edern's with it, and he nodded, putting his mouth against the rope that bound their wrists together.

"Not yet," whispered Edern. "Wait until we reach some trees where I can hide. It looks so desolate out there."

Gereint, who had overheard them, said softly, "You are fast, Edern. You can escape. But will we be rescued? Will you come back for us?"

"Of course. All of you." Edern looked at the shadowy faces around him. "All," he repeated. And then he turned to the cage. The kidnappers had been discussing Beri, he realized. "In two days she will be off our hands," they had said.

Soon, it would be too late to rescue the girl in the cage.

CHAPTER 10
"You Are a King!"

Summer had arrived, but in the mountainous country where Timoken found himself, the nights were still chilly. One morning, as he and Gabar were walking along a narrow mountain track, they heard a long, wailing call. It was in a language that Timoken had never heard, but there was no mistaking the desperate urgency in the voice.

Timoken had been leading Gabar, rather than riding him, and now he dropped the reins and, kneeling on the ground, looked over the edge of the track. At first, he could see nothing, and then, far below, he made out the small figure of a boy. He was sitting on a ledge that jutted out a yard or so above a fast and furious river. The boy had thick copper-colored hair and a face that looked all the paler for the dark blood that streamed from his nose.

"I fell!" The boy looked up at Timoken. "Can you help me?"

A strange language, thought Timoken. But he could understand it. He withdrew his head and tried to think what to do.

"Please don't leave me, I beg you!" called the boy. "I think my arm is broken, and I cannot swim."

How did he think anyone could rescue him? It was an almost sheer drop down to the ledge. Even with a rope it would be impossible to rescue the boy if he had a broken arm. Timoken had no choice. He would have to fly.

"Gabar, don't move!" Timoken commanded. "This track is dangerous."

Gabar gave a loud snort and stamped his foot, sending a shower of rocks bouncing down the mountainside.

"HELP!" came a cry.

"I'm coming," called Timoken. He launched himself off the track and floated gently down to the ledge where the boy was sitting. For a moment they gazed, astonished, at each other. And then the strange boy asked, "Do all Africans fly?"

"No," replied Timoken. "Do all your people have fiery hair and . . . and marks across their faces?"

"Only some," said the boy. "My father and my brothers are all freckle-faced."

A cascade of stones came tumbling down behind him and he yelped, "Can you lift me, African? Can you fly with me?"

"I can lift camels," said Timoken, putting his arms around the boy's waist. Lifting him carefully, Timoken easily flew up to the track.

Gabar, surprised by the sudden appearance of the two boys, stepped away nervously. One of his back feet slipped off the side of the track and, with a rumble of stones, the camel disappeared over the edge, bellowing with fear.

Without hesitation, Timoken dropped the boy on the ground and flew after Gabar. He tried to catch him as he fell, but the camel was heavy and laden with bags. He dropped like a stone into the fast-flowing river, his desperate voice gurgling up through the water in rings of muddy bubbles.

Timoken plunged after him. The river was thick with weeds and mud, but he could feel Gabar's shaggy hair just beneath the surface and, looping his arms around the camel's neck, he pulled with every ounce of his strength. Gabar thrashed in the water for a moment and then, all at once, his body sagged and he sank down to the riverbed.

Timoken pressed his face against the camel's head and, keeping his mouth closed, he hummed into his ear. "You will not drown. You cannot drown. You are my family, and I am yours. Up, Gabar. UP!"

The camel's head drooped, but Timoken would not let go. His lungs were bursting and he longed to take a breath, but he rubbed the shaggy neck and hummed into his ear again, "Up, Gabar! Up, up, up."

Gabar did not move. Timoken thought, briefly, of the boy he had just rescued. What would he do now, if Timoken drowned with the camel? Because he would drown if Gabar did not move. He could not bring himself to leave his oldest friend, his family.

There was a movement beneath him. The camel was struggling to his feet. With a surge of hope, Timoken pulled Gabar's head upward, up to the surface of the water where they both took long gasps of air, and then up again, the camel's heavy body struggling out of the river while Timoken shouted encouragement. Gabar's big feet kicked themselves free of the water, and Timoken lifted him into the air. Now they were flying, their grunts and cries of delight filling the air.

They landed on the track with a bit of a scramble. Gabar sank to his knees, water pouring from the bags tied to his saddle. Timoken lifted the bags off the camel as fast as he could. Only when he had made sure that Gabar was safe did he notice the red-haired boy, gaping at him, almost in horror.

Timoken grinned at the boy. "I thought I had lost him," he said. "He is my family, you see!"

The boy just stared at Timoken. At last he said, "What are you?"

"I am just a boy," Timoken replied.

The boy shook his head vigorously. "No, you are a king, I think." He pointed to the gold band embedded in Timoken's thick hair, the crown that had never left his head. "A magician-king," the boy added, dropping his voice.

Timoken could not help laughing. He still felt so happy to have rescued Gabar. "My name is Timoken, and I suppose I would be a king," he admitted, "if I had a kingdom. But it is all gone." He fell silent for a moment and then said, brightly, "We must find somewhere safe to dry ourselves and talk."

The boy went first. He limped a little, from a twisted ankle, but pressed on in a very determined way, his free hand holding his injured arm against his side. Gabar followed the boy, placing his feet carefully on the rough track. And Timoken came last, so that he could watch the others. He dragged the saddle and the wet bags behind him, and he thought of the moon cloak, and how he could use it to warm Gabar's back and perhaps, even, to mend the boy's arm.

Luckily, they did not have to walk far before they came to a small grove of trees growing in an old quarry. There was room to spread the wet clothes and for Gabar to sit in the sun and dry himself.

The boy's arm was not broken after all, but badly bruised. Timoken gave him some water and then, a little self-consciously, he lit a fire. Although the sun was out, the wind was chilly and Gabar was still shivering from fright and the cold.

The boy watched Timoken for a while, and then he said, "My uncle can do that!"

"He can use his fingers to . . . ?"

"Light a fire, yes. But he cannot fly."

Timoken began to spread his possessions in the sunlight. He gave the boy some dried meat, and they sat watching the flames and each other before Timoken eventually asked the boy's name.

"Edern," the boy replied and then, unable to keep quiet any longer, he began to explain how he had come to be in such a dangerous place and so far from home.

"I come from a land many, many days away," said Edern. "My father is a poet and I lived in a castle in much splendor, because the prince of our country values poets even above soldiers. One evening a group of monks came to the castle, begging for shelter. It was our duty to let them in. But that night they stole up to the room where my three friends and I were sleeping. Before we could cry out, they had gagged us and bound our hands and feet. They carried us out of the castle, past two guards who were sleeping, drugged, no doubt." Edern's mouth formed a grim line. "We kicked and struggled but those men were no holy monks; they were built like oxen, brutal, powerful, and cruel. They put us in a covered wagon and drove us to the sea, where a ship was waiting. We were carried aboard in sacks, like so much rubbish, and thrown into the hold. There were other children there, weeping and groaning. Some lay very still, too still."

Edern rubbed his bruised arm and stared at the sky, shading his face with his hand. "When we came to this land, wherever it is, we were loaded onto carts. But some of the children got sick. They were thrown out to die on the road, like dogs."

"But you escaped," said Timoken, trying to sound cheerful. "And now you are on your way home."

Edern shook his head. "Not without my friends. I promised to go back and rescue them, when I found someone to help."

"Well, you have found help," said Timoken. "But who are these men who are not monks? Did they kidnap you for a ransom? And were your families unable to pay the price?"

Edern leaned forward. "We were to be slaves," he said in a low voice. "Rich men in the East will pay a fortune for slaves with pale skin and yellow hair" — he touched his head with a rueful grin — "and even more, it seems, for boys with hair like mine."

"Slaves?" said Timoken in horror. "Where are your friends now? Have you come far?"

"Not far," said Edern. "This track will soon descend through woods into a wide valley. The false monks hold my friends in a barn there in the trees. Every night we were roped together by our hands. I was at the end of the line, next to my friend, Peredur. Peredur is renowned for his sharp teeth; they are like the teeth of a wolf." Edern opened his mouth in a wide grin and pointed to his incisors. "And so he gnawed the rope between us, and when his jaw began to ache, I gnawed, and between us we chewed right through the rope. As soon as I was free, I stood on Peredur's shoulders and climbed through a hole in the roof. It was but a short jump to the ground."

"Were there no guards?"

"All the false monks were asleep in a stone house beside the barn. The dogs were our guards; three great brindled hounds that set up a great barking at the slightest noise."

"And they did not see or hear you?"

"They did. But we had saved a little of the meat that evening, and hidden it beneath the stones where we sat. I threw it to the dogs and they let me pass, but their first warning barks had woken the false monks, and one came stumbling out of the house. He must have thought the dogs were eating a rabbit, or some other creature, for he cursed them for their noise and went back to bed."

Timoken's mind began to race. He was confident that he could rescue Edern's friends, but he had to plan his actions. "How many of you are there?" he asked.

"There were twenty or more. But only twelve of us survived the sickness. We must rescue them soon," Edern said anxiously. "Tomorrow they will be on the move again."

"Perhaps they have gone already," Timoken said. "Would those brigands stay another night in the same place?"

"They were waiting for someone," said Edern. "We heard them talking. One of the girls was to be collected today. She is in a cage." He paused for a moment and added, with a frown, "I am afraid for her, Timoken. I am afraid for all my friends, but the way those false monks talked, I think they expect a large sum of money for this girl, and so they will guard her very closely. Perhaps we cannot rescue her."

"Nothing is impossible," said Timoken. "I have a plan already. We will wait for moonlight."

That evening he packed the bags for traveling. Everything had dried in the sun, even the woolen blankets. Gabar had thoroughly recovered, and ate a hearty meal of dried fruit and grass before dozing off. Timoken unfolded the moon cloak and laid it under the trees. The boy watched, his expression a mixture of wonder and curiosity.

"What is that?"

Timoken hesitated. Should he tell Edern the truth? The boy already knew so much about him, what did it matter? Timoken trusted him. He was certain that Edern was not the one whom the ring had warned him about.

"It is made from the silk of the last moon spider," he said at last. "I call it the moon cloak, and it will protect us. We must get some sleep before we set off to rescue your friends." Timoken lay beneath the moon cloak and beckoned to the boy.

After a moment of uncertainty, Edern crawled in beside him. The red-haired boy was soon asleep, but Timoken lay staring up at the night sky. Where was the moon? They needed a good light if they were to rescue all the children and escape. He had been gazing at a pale splinter of light for several seconds before he realized what it was. The new moon was rising in the eastern sky.

Quickly rolling from beneath the moon cloak, Timoken ran to the bags that were piled beside Gabar. The Alixir was kept in a small pouch of red calfskin. But it was not there.

"It must have been lost in the water," Timoken said to himself, "when poor Gabar fell in the river." He looked again at the thin slice of moon and shivered. He had found no home as yet, but he was going to grow. He would be like other mortals. The prospect was exciting, and a little alarming. He had been eleven years old for more than two centuries; in less than another eleven years, he would be a man.

CHAPTER 11
The Angel on the Roof

Edern woke up. A thick blanket of clouds obscured the stars, and yet there was a light in the grove where he lay.

He could see the camel, its head lowered and its eyes closed. He could see the branches of the trees, spread like a canopy above his head. He sat up, and light rippled across the cloak that covered his legs. It was like seeing the moon reflected in water. Edern ran his hand lightly over the glimmering threads. They were so soft, he could hardly feel them. Beside him, Timoken stirred in his sleep; the band of gold around his head glinted in the gentle light.

"A king," Edern said to himself. Something his father had said came into his head: "To be a king is an honor and a burden. He cannot show fear, and he cannot shoulder the huge weight of his responsibilities without our support. Never forget that."

Edern looked at his sleeping companion. *I won't forget,* he thought.

He shook Timoken's shoulder and the African woke with a start. "I have never slept so deeply." He yawned and stretched his arms.

"I think we should go now," said Edern.

"Of course!" Timoken exclaimed. He went over to the camel and began to load him up.

"It is night," grunted Gabar.

"I'm sorry. We have a task to perform — a rescue!" Timoken lit a small lamp and hung it at the front of the saddle.

Gabar wearily lifted his rump. "Rescue?" he snorted. "At night?"

"Yes. And don't get up yet. We have to climb on your back."

"Two again," grumbled Gabar.

Timoken smiled. "We weigh hardly anything." He got into the saddle and called Edern over, telling him to climb up behind him.

When they were ready, Gabar raised himself to his feet and, at a touch of the reins, began to walk down the mountain track. It had widened out into a rough road, and on either side trees grew thickly, keeping the camel safe from another tumble.

As they traveled, Timoken described his plan to Edern. They would stop a little way before reaching the barn, so the dogs would not hear them. When he was quite sure no animal had been alerted, Timoken would fly into the trees above the buildings. He would talk softly to the dogs, commanding them to be silent, and then he would ask the horses to be quiet and steady while he untied the ropes that tethered them to the trees.

"They keep the saddlery in a hut beside the stone house," Edern said. "Shall I saddle the horses while you are freeing my friends?"

"No," said Timoken firmly. "I will do it. I will call to you when all is safe. If you do not hear from me before dawn, it means I have failed, so you must find some other route, and continue alone on Gabar."

It had not occurred to Edern that Timoken might fail. He could find nothing to say, except, "I understand."

"Treat my camel well," said Timoken. "He is family."

"I will," Edern said huskily. "But you will not fail."

They reached a sharp turn in the road and Edern said, "We are close to the barn. It is maybe two hundred strides away."

Timoken guided Gabar into the trees at the side of the road. He took the moon cloak from a bag and swung it across his head. Edern watched in awe as the clouds rolled back and starlight filtered down through the trees.

Timoken leaped from the camel's back, and the last Edern saw of him was a pale shape, floating high in the trees. The moon cloak streamed behind him, like a pair of silvery wings.

The girl in the cage looked up through the hole in the roof and saw what she thought was an angel. One of the boys saw it, too. "Look! Look!" he cried.

Beri knew they must be quiet if the angel was to rescue them. "Shh!" she hissed. She could smell fire.

Other children were waking up now. The angel perched on the roof and looked down at them. He put a finger to his lips and whispered, "Hush!"

Silence fell. The angel had a dark face and wore a thin gold crown. The children were a little afraid of him. They had never seen an African before. Beri had seen many. Now that he was close, she doubted that he was an angel, even when he dropped lightly to the ground, as though he were borne on wings.

Timoken whispered quickly to the children while he severed their bonds. He told them he could not remove the heavy chains across the door, but he could carry them up, one by one, through the roof. They would find horses saddled and ready, but they would have to ride two to a horse. When they were all free, he turned his attention to the cage.

"How will you open this?" asked the girl, shaking the iron bars.

Timoken grinned. "Wait and see." He walked around the cage, stroking his chin like an old man.

The others began to whisper urgently. "Please, get us out. The false monks will hear. They'll catch us before we can ride away."

Timoken turned to them, frowning. "Hush!" His tone was severe. "Climb on each other's shoulders if you can't wait!" He walked around the cage again. The door was padlocked; the key, presumably, in one of the false monks' pockets.

The little pearl-handled knife would not do. All Timoken had were his hands. He put his ringed finger on the padlock and murmured, "Help me, ring! Melt! Click! Open!"

The girl couldn't understand him. "What are you doing?" she asked.

Timoken was too absorbed to answer her. His finger felt as though it was burning. The pain was almost unbearable. And now he thought his whole hand was being boiled, but he kept his finger on the padlock until, suddenly, with a loud *click*, it opened and fell to the ground.

The girl stared at Timoken in astonishment. "So you are a magician, not an angel," she said. Cautiously, she pushed at the cage door.

"Quickly!" urged Timoken. "Get out!"

The moment the girl stepped out of the cage, Timoken seized her around the waist and flew up through the hole with her. His feet had hardly touched the roof before he was floating gently down to the ground.

The girl saw flames billowing up in front of the stone house. Timoken had built a pyre against the door and set it alight. The false monks could be heard shouting inside the house. There was only one window and that too was engulfed in flames.

"They will burn," said Beri, with satisfaction.

"No," Timoken told her. "It will rain and the fire will die."

"How do you know?" Puzzled, the girl stared at his solemn face.

"Find a horse and wait for one of the others," he commanded, giving her a little shove in the direction of the house.

Some of the other children had already managed to climb onto the roof and were even now jumping to the ground. Timoken flew up to collect the others and remained on the roof while they found their horses. As soon as they were all mounted, he gave a loud bellow and Gabar came thumping through the trees with Edern on his back.

"Edern!" cried the Britons. "You found a camel."

"A camel and a friend," Edern replied.

Timoken leaped from the barn roof and landed lightly in the camel saddle. "Go now," he called to the others. "We will follow."

The six horses took off immediately, their riders calling loudly to one another, keen to put a distance between themselves and their captors.

"What are we waiting for?" Edern asked anxiously.

"There is another horse," said Timoken. "He pulls the wagon. I untied the rope that tethered him, but he would not move. The other horses listened to me. They were happy to obey, but not this one. If we left him, the false monks could follow us."

They rode into the woods at the back of the house. The big horse was standing under a tree. He had not moved since Timoken had spoken to him.

Gabar seemed uneasy. He was reluctant to go too close. But Timoken urged him forward until they were only three strides away from the horse. He was a huge beast, jet black, with hooves bigger than a camel's foot.

"Go now," said Timoken in a rough snort. "You are free."

A deep and dreadful sound came from the horse. It was more of a roar than a neigh. It made no sense to Timoken. "Horse, why won't you go?" he asked.

The great beast pawed the ground. It looked as though it was about to charge at them, and the camel stepped back nervously. The black horse thrust out its head and rolled back its lips, revealing its huge teeth. Then, from its throat, came a snarl that had no meaning.

"Let's go," cried Edern. "I have never seen such an evil creature."

Timoken was shaken. Until now he had understood every animal that he had met. They all had a language, but not this beast. *It is possessed by an evil thing*, he thought. It worried him that, even here, wickedness existed, when he thought he had left it far behind. He gave the camel's reins a light tug and grunted, "Go, Gabar. Go like the wind!"

Gabar was only too happy to obey.

As they passed the stone house, Timoken saw that the flames had reached the roof, and burning rafters were crashing into the building.

"They cannot follow us now," muttered Edern.

But Timoken could not bear the false monks' screams. Waving his arms at the sky, he called for rain, and within seconds, rain-drops the size of pebbles came tumbling down on their heads.

Gabar gave a snort of disgust and galloped down the road.

Timoken did not stop the rain until he was sure that enough water had fallen to douse the fire.

Edern was disappointed. "They will follow us now," he grum-bled. "They have the wagon and that brute of a horse. And they have weapons. When they catch up with us, we are done for."

Timoken just laughed. "If they follow us, then I will bring thunder and lightning on their heads. Don't be so gloomy, Edern. I have weapons, too, even though you cannot see them."

Edern grinned. "So you have. We'd better catch up with the others; they may be in need of your special weapons."

"Let's find them, Gabar," said Timoken. And Gabar's pace increased.

They trotted across the valley, past small hamlets and lonely farmhouses, through dense woods, over bridges, and below a castle that stood proud on a rocky hill. But there was no sign of the eleven children, and Timoken began to fear that they had been caught again, by bandits or worse. The children had no protection but their wits.

"Peredur Sharptooth has wits as well as teeth," said Edern, almost as though he had read Timoken's thoughts.

"Then let us hope that his wits are as sharp as his teeth," said Timoken.

In spite of the danger, Edern found himself laughing.

CHAPTER 12
Poisoned

The next day they came to a village where something odd
had happened. Something ominous. The usual scent of
woodsmoke was absent. There were other smells: death and
decay. Night was falling fast but the houses were all in darkness.
Not a light showed anywhere. The village stood in a great, hollow silence.

Timoken was reluctant to stop. He was afraid for the eleven
children, and wanted to find them before it became too dark. But
Gabar demanded a rest. He had seen a stone trough standing
beneath a pump in the center of the village, and he made toward
it. As the camel bent his head to drink, Timoken suddenly jerked
the reins, forcing Gabar away from the water.

The camel bellowed furiously. "I am thirsty. Why will you
not let me drink?"

"Look at the water, Gabar! Look!"

The reflected light from Timoken's lamp made the water sparkle. To Gabar, it looked delicious.

"What's wrong?" Edern peered around Timoken to get a better look. "Why won't you let the camel drink?"

"Because someone has poisoned the water." Even as he spoke, Timoken realized that Edern could not see the thin green mist rising from the trough; a mist filled with swimming shapes, diminutive forms with grotesque features. They were grinning at him, their twisted faces full of malice.

"How do you know?" Edern asked in a puzzled voice. "How can you tell that the water is poisoned?"

"I can see them," Timoken said simply.

"Them?"

"Demons."

Gabar felt something now. He could not see the tiny forms, but he could sense them, and he began to back away.

Edern could see nothing, yet he knew that Timoken must be believed. "What shall we do?"

"Perhaps the whole village has been poisoned," Timoken said thoughtfully. "Perhaps they are all dead, but then some might have lived."

Edern looked at the houses, which stood shadowed and silent in the gathering darkness. "Should we go and look?" he said, a little fearfully.

"We must."

Gabar knelt and the two boys climbed down. The first house they entered was quite empty. So was the next. In both houses there was food on the table, a water pitcher, and several tankards. The pitcher was empty. So were the tankards. When they found no one at home in the third house, they began to think that perhaps the villagers had been frightened away, and not poisoned after all.

Timoken returned to the trough. He steeled himself to look at the water again. The tiny demons were still there, floating in their pea green vapor. Cautiously, he poked his ringed finger into the mist. The demons he touched shrieked with pain and shot upward; pinpricks of lime green light, hurtling through the dark sky.

"I saw them," cried Edern, enthralled by the shooting lights. "What did you do?"

"I am not sure," answered Timoken. "But they are not smiling at me now." On the other side of the trough he could just make out a large building, set back from the others. It was a meetinghouse, perhaps, or the home of an important village elder. Were all the villagers in there? Had they gone to seek advice, for an illness brought on by the infected water? Timoken was about to investigate the large house when Edern suddenly clutched his arm.

"Listen," Edern whispered.

A boy's voice came drifting through the air. It was very clear and sweet, and it was singing in Edern's language.

"Gereint!" cried Edern. "I know his voice so well. He is our prince's favorite singer." He ran toward the house where the singing could be heard. Timoken followed him.

The door was open and the two boys ran in. Candles flickered on a rough table where nine children sat, their faces white and terrified. But when Edern and Timoken walked into the light, the children jumped up, smiling with relief.

Running to Edern, Peredur cried, "We thought you were lost, or caught again by those false monks."

"You are not all here," said Timoken solemnly. "Where are the others?"

Peredur's face fell. "We think they are dying." He stood back and pointed to a dark corner, where two children lay on a mattress, a boy and a girl. The others had covered them with their jerkins, but the sick children looked very close to death. Their eyes were closed, and they did not appear to be breathing.

Another boy approached Timoken. He was smaller than Peredur, and his hair was very blond. "I was singing to them," he said, almost apologetically. "I thought it would ease their journey into heaven."

"They are not dead." Timoken walked over to the mattress and knelt beside the children. "He is warm," he said, taking the boy's hand. "What happened?"

"They rode ahead of us," said Peredur. "Henri was always urging his horse to go faster, and poor Isabelle, sitting behind him in her long dress, was always scared of falling off. When we reached the village, we found their horse tied to a post, and then we saw Henri and Isabelle; they were both lying beside the pump. Their lips were green and slimy, their faces pale as death."

"We thought it must be the water," said Gereint, the singer. "So we decided not to touch it."

"You were wise," muttered Timoken. He whirled through the door and ran to Gabar, who was standing patiently outside.

"Water?" Gabar inquired, as Timoken pulled the moon cloak from a bag.

"Later, Gabar," said Timoken. "The water in the trough is poisoned; be grateful that I stopped you from drinking it."

"Always grateful, Family," the camel grunted as Timoken ran back into the house.

He threw the moon cloak over the sick children and sat beside them. Edern brought a candle and held it up so that the light fell on the sick children's faces. The others gathered behind him, whispering anxiously. The moon cloak glimmered in the soft light, its threads like a pattern of stars.

"What is that thing?"

Timoken recognized the caged girl's voice. She sounded suspicious. He was not sure how to explain the moon cloak.

"Magician, tell me what you are doing." Her voice was gentler now. "I trust you, but I want to know."

Timoken took a breath and, lifting a corner of the web, said, "I call this the moon cloak. It is made from the web of the last moon spider. It keeps me safe and, sometimes, it can heal." He translated his words for the others.

The children behind him murmured in awe. The sound grew to a buzz of excitement as Henri turned his face and groaned.

"He's coming 'round," said Peredur.

They waited expectantly, watching Henri's face. Suddenly, he sat up and groaned, "I'm going to be sick!" Although the Britons didn't understand him, they had a very good idea what was about to happen and leaped back like the others, as Henri bent over and retched. A green liquid pooled on the earthen floor. Only Timoken saw the demons writhing in the puddle and slowly dying. In a few seconds, the green liquid had seeped into the earth, leaving only a small, damp patch.

"It's you!" said Henri, looking up into Timoken's face. "Did you save me yet again?"

Timoken grinned. "No. The moon cloak did that."

Henri frowned at the glimmering web. "Aw!" He swung his legs onto the floor and stood up, letting the moon cloak float down beside the girl. "Oh, Isabelle!" Henri's hand flew to his mouth. "She's still sick. And it's my fault. I made her drink the water. It was poisoned, wasn't it?"

"You idiot!" said one of the French boys. He was tall and thin, with a mop of blond curls. "Why are you always racing ahead?"

"I'm sorry, Gerard. I can't help myself. I did not mean. Oh . . ." Henri covered his face with his hands. "Will she die?"

"No," Timoken said firmly.

"She's opened her eyes!" cried Edern.

All at once, Isabelle sat bolt upright. Long strands of damp hair clung to her face, and she looked wildly about her, not understanding where she was or how she got there. "Oooooh!" she moaned, leaning across the mattress.

The others backed even farther away as Isabelle retched, and a familiar green liquid spilled onto the floor.

"What has happened to me?" cried the poor girl.

Ignoring the small demons dying at his feet, Timoken crouched beside her and laid a hand on her shoulder. "You were poisoned," he said gently. "But now you are better. You are with your friends."

Isabelle looked up. A broad smile lit her face and she said, "You are the boy who rescued us. We thought you were lost."

"No. Not lost," said Timoken. "I am never lost." He stood up and the other French children crowded around Isabelle, exclaiming with joy and relief. She got to her feet and lifted the web, gazing at the glittering patterns.

"It's magic," Henri told her. "It saved us. I'm sorry, Isabelle. It was all my fault."

While the French children chattered eagerly to one another, the Britons were searching for food. They had already eaten a loaf of bread they had found on the table.

"I am going to the big house," Timoken told them. "The villagers may have gone there."

"No!" One of the Britons swung around. He was older than the others, taller and broader. His hair was not even blond; it was a rich brown. Perhaps he had been stolen for the color of his eyes, which were a very pale blue.

"Why should we not go there, Mabon?" asked Edern.

"It is . . . it is full of dead people," Mabon said gravely. "We went there first, thinking that only a village elder would live in such a grand house."

"All dead?" murmured Timoken.

"All," said Mabon.

"They probably went there for help when the sickness came upon them," said Peredur.

Timoken lowered his head. It suddenly felt very heavy. "I was too late," he mumbled.

The children had found some dried beans and a few vegetables. There would be enough food for everyone, but there was nothing to drink, and they dared not fill the cooking pot with water from the pump.

"It is going to rain," said Timoken. "Bring every jug, every bowl and tankard outside. We will soon have water."

The children stared at Timoken suspiciously, but before any questions could be asked, Edern said, "Come on, everyone. You heard what Timoken said. It is going to rain."

There was a moment of silence, and then everyone was

grabbing a container of some sort. They followed Timoken outside and, holding up their jugs and pots and tankards, watched, astonished, as the African whirled the moon cloak above his head, and rain tumbled out of the dark sky in never-ending bucketfuls. While it was still raining, Timoken ran into some of the other houses and brought out more bowls and jugs. Eventually, he found what he was looking for — a huge cauldron. He dragged it to the entrance of a stable and called to Gabar.

"I thought you had forgotten me," the camel grumbled as he came pounding over to the stable.

"Quick, get inside." Timoken ordered. "Next, you'll be blaming me for soaking you. When the cauldron is full of water, you only have to poke out your head to take a drink."

"It is all very well," Gabar muttered, easing himself under the low roof. "But thank you, Family."

When Timoken returned to the house, he found that the children had filled the cooking pot hanging in the fireplace.

As he approached them, it came to him that these children knew almost everything about him now, and he remembered his sister's warning. Yet how could he have kept his secrets? *What would you have done, Zobayda?* he wondered. A sharp pain traveled through his ringed finger, up his arm, and into his very heart. Only one of the children noticed that he was shaking.

"What is it, Timoken?" asked the girl from the cage. "Are you in pain?"

In a second, the pain had gone, and Timoken was able to answer truthfully, "It is nothing."

"Are you sure?" She touched his arm. In the candlelit room her eyes looked a deep violet blue. She was still a child, but Timoken saw that she was already beautiful. The ribbons in her hair were made of fine silk, he noticed, and her dress was edged with gold lace. *She must, indeed, be very special,* he thought. He was about to ask her name when she said, "I am called Beri."

When the thick soup was cooked, the children ladled it into bowls and then squeezed together onto the benches at either side of the table. Some were beginning to gobble it up, even before they had sat down.

"What was that?" Gereint looked at the door.

Timoken had heard it, too. A soft, shuffling sound. It was followed by a kind of scratching. Slowly, the latch was lifted and the door creaked open.

An ancient face appeared, so wrinkled and bony it was difficult to know if it was a man or a woman, but as more of its form moved into the room, they saw that it must be a woman. Beneath her gray shawl, her back was bent, and her garments hung loosely on her scrawny frame. The hem of her dress was torn and ragged from being dragged through the mud and stepped upon.

"Children!" she croaked. "Dead or ghosts?"

"We are not dead." Timoken stood up.

The old woman stared at him in horror. "It's you!" she cried. "You are the one he was looking for!"

Timoken shuddered under the accusing gaze of the old woman. "Who is looking for me?" he asked in a small voice.

The dry, wrinkled lips worked furiously, trying to utter a word. At last she managed it. "The sorcerer!" The word came out in a wheezy gasp as she crumpled to the ground.

CHAPTER 13
The Sorcerer

Mabon and Peredur carried the old woman over to the mattress and laid her down. Her eyelids fluttered, and she drew a deep, rasping breath.

Timoken knelt beside her. "Madame, who is this sorcerer?"

She gave a bitter laugh. "Who knows?" Her next breath brought on a coughing fit, and when she had recovered, she said, "I saw it all, but then I went to sleep, and so it was too late to warn them."

When she began to cough again, Marie, one of the French girls, brought her a tankard of water. The girl was smaller than the others, only six or seven years old. The old woman cried, "Poison!" and struck Marie's hand, sending the tankard crashing to the floor.

"It is pure rainwater," said Timoken.

"Oh?" The woman's eyes narrowed suspiciously.

"We have been drinking it, and, as you can see"—Timoken spread his hands and looked at the others—"we are all still alive."

The old woman uttered a wary "Hm!" And then she said, "They all died, you know. The others. When I woke up I could hear moanings and groanings from the other houses. I saw men and women and little children rolling and retching up to Monsieur Clement's house. He is a physician, and his potions have cured many ailments. Not this time. Monsieur Clement was dead already." She began to cough again, and this time she accepted the water that Marie offered her.

Timoken watched her drain the tankard. He wanted to know more about the sorcerer, but did not like to press her. The water seemed to revive her and she sat up, wiping her whiskery chin. Edern brought her a bowl of soup, and she slurped it down greedily, smacking her lips between every sip.

The children watched in silence, waiting for the old woman to speak again. At length, she handed Edern the empty bowl and sat back against the wall, folding her arms across her chest.

"Please, Madame . . . ," Timoken began.

"Grüner," she snapped. "Adèle Grüner."

"Can you tell us what happened here?" asked Timoken.

"Don't stare at me," Madame Grüner complained. "Go and sit down, all of you."

Timoken motioned the others to sit. He told them that Madame Grüner might be persuaded to describe what had happened.

The French children clustered around the table, while the Britons sat cross-legged on the floor. Beri came and knelt beside Timoken. "You will have to explain her words to some of us," she said.

Timoken nodded.

Madame Grüner had already begun to talk. She mumbled and wheezed her way through the events that led up to the death of her village, while Timoken relayed her words to Beri and the Britons in their different languages. Within a few seconds he had mastered this process so well that the others hardly noticed it. His words reached them in one seamless story.

The old woman lived at the far end of the village. Three days ago she was collecting sticks in the wood behind her house, when five horsemen rode up. They were leading another horse, a huge black beast that snorted fire and whose great hooves made the earth tremble as he passed. Four of the strangers had a green look about them; their limbs were long and appeared to have no joints. No knees, no wrists, no elbows. They wore fine clothes and their green cloaks were lined with fur, but their faces . . . "Their faces . . ." Madame Grüner stopped speaking and rubbed her eyes. It was as though she were trying to rub away the memory. All at once her hands dropped to her sides, and she said, "Their faces were not right."

The fifth horseman was not much older than Timoken. He had brown-gold hair and eyes the color of dark green olives. Madame Grüner knew this because he stopped and spoke to her.

He asked if she had seen an African boy on a camel. She had laughed at him because she had only heard of such things but never seen them, and would not expect to in her lifetime. Her laughter annoyed the boy and, without warning, he pulled out a whip and struck her hands. She cried out in pain, dropping the bundle of sticks. The boy merely smiled. Leaning from his horse, he said coldly, "Old woman, this is not a joke." Then he turned his horse and led the group into the village.

"And now I have seen things that I never thought I would," murmured Madame Grüner. "A camel in our stable and an African wearing a crown."

Timoken awkwardly touched his head. He had forgotten to wear his hood. "How did they die, Madame Grüner, all those people?"

She took another sip of water and went on, "When I got back to the village, I saw Monsieur Clement talking to the strangers. The boy was shouting, and my neighbor told me that there had been an argument. The boy sorcerer said that an African on a camel was on his way to the village." She pointed a bony finger at Timoken. "You!"

Timoken frowned. Without a doubt she was right. He twisted the ring, remembering the forest-jinni's warning. A viridee had become human. Timoken knew what he wanted: the moon cloak. And he would kill to get it. "I hope I was not the cause of all those deaths." Timoken's voice was so low, only the girl beside him heard it.

"Monsieur Clement was a brave man." The old woman's watery eyes spilled tears down her furrowed cheeks. "My neighbor told me that when the boy commanded that the African should be caught and imprisoned, Monsieur Clement refused. He was adamant. Visitors would always be welcome in the village, he said, unless their intentions were evil. It was his duty to offer hospitality, not harm. And he looked at the crowd and asked, 'Am I not right, my friends?' And they all agreed, very loudly, whereupon the boy shouted a curse at him. When he and his companions rode off, I heard him call out that we had made the wrong choice."

"And they came back," said Timoken.

Madame Grüner nodded. Her hands plucked at her skirt and she began to mumble incoherently. Timoken took one of her hands. He only meant to calm her, but when he touched her dry skin and looked into her faded gray eyes, he began to see what she had seen in the village, three nights ago. It was dark, but a lamp burned outside Monsieur Clement's house. A boy stood beside the pump. He dropped a stone into the water trough, a shining stone that gave the water an eerie gleam. The boy began to speak. His language was harsh and ugly, his voice too deep for a boy. *A spell*, thought Timoken. Before he left, the boy put his fingers on the pump, and for a few seconds the handle glowed like a hot poker. And the boy smiled.

Timoken heard Beri's voice, very close, saying, "How can you make sense of all that babbling?" And he realized that he had not been listening to Madame Grüner, but describing a scene that was in her head.

"I was with her," he said, and, beside him, he felt Beri shiver, slightly.

Madame Grüner continued to babble, and once more the things that she saw began to swim before Timoken's eyes.

It was the morning after the boy had thrown the stone. The sun had not yet risen and no one had come to the pump. But Madame Grüner was still awake, and she heard the clatter of hooves on the cobblestones. Two monks rode into the village. They dismounted and looked about them. Seeing a stable, they walked stealthily toward it. Their movements were furtive, their faces guilty. Horse thieves, no doubt. Before Madame Grüner could cry a warning, the boy sorcerer appeared, and she was afraid.

The boy spoke to the monks and they replied. Madame Grüner was too far away to hear them, but Timoken watched their lips and understood. The monks were looking for a horse to pull their wagon. The boy offered them an animal that was stronger than any horse on earth. But there was a condition. They must capture an African who rode a camel.

"And then what?" asked one of the monks. "In three days we have to deliver certain goods to a trader in the city of St. Fleur."

The boy shrugged. "Make your delivery. And then bring me the African. The horse will find me, wherever I am. He is a beast of my own making."

The monks frowned, not quite believing the boy. He disappeared from view, and when he returned he was leading a great black horse. The monks looked incredulous. Before the boy handed the horse over, he spoke to it, all the while stroking the beast's nose. He passed the reins to one of the monks, and warned them not to drink the water from the pump. As he said this, he looked directly at Madame Grüner's window. An icy light streamed from his green eyes. Its touch was so painful that she had to cover her face. She dropped to the floor and fell into a deep sleep. When she woke up, everyone else in the village was dying or dead.

Madame Grüner's head drooped. Her eyes were closed and she appeared to be asleep.

Timoken released the old woman's hand. He rubbed the back of his neck and shook his shoulders. He felt so tired, he wanted to lay his head beside the old woman's and sleep. "Did you hear all that?" he asked the others.

"We heard," said Edern. "The black horse was possessed, as we thought. Why does the sorcerer want you, Timoken?"

"It is not me that he wants." Timoken lifted the moon cloak from the mattress where Isabelle had dropped it. "It is this. And perhaps something that I no longer have."

They waited for him to say more and so, reluctantly, he told them about the Alixir that had been lost in the river. He told them about the secret kingdom and the way that his father and mother had died. He told them about the viridees, and, last of all, about his sister, Zobayda. When he had finished, the only sound in the room came from the old woman, who was quietly snoring.

Timoken's arm had begun to throb again. And again, there was a light tug at his heart. "I think we should sleep now," he said. "Tomorrow we will decide what to do."

He could feel the children's eyes on him, but still no one spoke. What could they say after such a story? *I have said it all, now*, thought Timoken, *or nearly all.* For more than two hundred years he had carried his story alone, but now children that he trusted knew it, too, and he felt lighter and happier for having shared it. The only thing that he had kept to himself was his age, his and Gabar's.

They set about preparing for bed. They would all sleep in the one room, they decided. It would be safer that way. The horses were brought in from the woods and stabled close to the house. There was plenty of hay for them, and enough left over to take into the house for pillows. Timoken hung the moon cloak across the door as a protection against the false monks, who might return. The candles were doused, and one by one the children curled up on the floor and went to sleep. Once again, the only sound in the room was Madame Grüner's quiet snoring.

Timoken had slept for only a few minutes before he found himself awake again. He had forgotten something.

Stepping carefully over the others, he unlatched the door and crept out.

Gabar was resting on the stable floor, but he was not asleep. Timoken removed the saddle and the heavy bags from his back. Finding some dried fruit in one of the bags, he laid it before the camel.

Gabar grunted his approval and ate the food.

"We have come a long way, you and I," said Timoken, crouching beside the camel. "And now we are going to grow old together."

Gabar said nothing, but when Timoken got up to leave, he grunted, "Family, please stay with me."

Timoken thought of the moon cloak, out of his reach now. But what did it matter? It would keep the children safe. He sank into the straw and, resting his head against the camel's warm body, fell asleep.

When Timoken entered the house the next morning a serious discussion was taking place. What was to be done with Madame Grüner? That was the question that worried everyone. The old woman was still asleep, and they did not want to frighten her awake.

Eventually, their noisy chatter woke her. For a moment, she scowled at them from under her heavy brows, and then she remembered what had happened and began to rock back and forth, moaning constantly.

"Madame, how can we help you?" asked Timoken.

The old woman stopped rocking. Frowning up at Timoken, she told him that she could not stay in a dead village. She would go to her cousin, who lived only a day's ride away. But there was a problem. Although the villagers' horses had not been given the poisoned water, she could no longer ride. Her hands were too frail to hold the reins, and she found it hard to sit upright.

"We will take you," said Timoken.

Martin, one of the French boys, offered to share his horse with Madame Grüner. He promised to hold her very tight, and to keep his horse under control so that she did not fall off.

It was quite a business, lifting the old woman up into the saddle. She caught her feet in her long skirt, twisted her hands in the reins, and protested loudly when Martin squeezed in behind her. But realizing it was the only way she was going to reach her cousin's village, she calmed down and, muttering directions, allowed Martin to lead the way out of the village.

They had found six extra horses, and so everyone had their own mount. The girls were very pleased about this. They looked different today. They had found clothes in the deserted houses and were now dressed as boys. Their hair was tucked into hoods attached to their short tunics. Having discarded their long dresses, they now wore woolen stockings, so their legs were free and they did not have to ride sidesaddle, which they found annoying and uncomfortable.

As the group approached a small village, half hidden in the woods, Henri began to look around him, studying the ancient trees. He twisted in the saddle, staring up at a towering pine and, with mounting surprise, declared that he thought he recognized the place, and that it was not so far from his home.

This caused a lot of excitement among the other French children. All at once their own homes seemed closer, and the possibility of seeing their parents before very long made some of them whoop with joy.

"Shush!" Madame Grüner commanded. "You will frighten everyone, and they will bar their doors."

And so they entered the village in silence, until Madame Grüner saw her cousin peeping out of a window. With a joyful cry, the old woman half slid and half tumbled off the horse and fell to the ground, while her cousin, a woman much younger than herself, rushed out and clasped her in her arms.

There followed such a babble of frantic conversation between the two, even the French children could not understand them.

Other people began to emerge from their houses. They stared in amazement at the camel. None of them had seen such a creature. But, at length, they motioned for the children to dismount and, climbing off their horses, the children stood grinning at the villagers, who all grinned back.

The cousin, Madame Magnier, invited everyone into her house, while the horses were taken to be fed and watered. Gabar, however, was left well alone.

"Well, Gabar," Timoken grunted softly. "I think you had better let me down, because I do not intend to fly."

He heard a woman say, "The African can only speak in grunts."

"On the contrary, Madame," said Timoken. "I can speak many languages. I was merely instructing my camel."

The woman gasped. When Gabar knelt, she suddenly saw Timoken's crown. "Forgive me," she said, blushing. "I am a foolish woman."

Timoken smiled. "You made a common mistake, Madame."

Soon the whole village knew the story of the boy sorcerer and the fatal poisonings. When they heard that all the children, except Timoken, had been kidnapped, they clutched their own children protectively, agreeing to never let them out of their sights.

That evening the visitors were given a grand meal in the village meetinghouse. While they ate, the villagers pressed them to tell their stories.

The children's accounts were listened to with outrage and horror. Several mothers stood up and piled even more food on their plates.

Madame Magnier's husband was a soldier, but after being wounded in battle he had returned home for good. He walked with a limp, but declared that his sword arm was still useful, and he offered to accompany the French children to the castle where Henri lived with his family.

"My father will make sure that the others are taken home, I promise you." Henri smiled around at the French children, who began to cheer and clap.

The Britons had been listening to all the chatter while they ate, but they could understand very little, and so when Monsieur Magnier leaned over the table and asked Edern where he wished to go, Edern merely shrugged and looked puzzled.

"He is asking you where you want to go from here," said Timoken.

"I go with you," Edern said quickly. He asked the other Britons.

"We stay together," said Peredur, "with you."

"And the girl there, who is not French?" asked Madame Magnier.

"Where do you want to go next?" Timoken asked Beri.

"Home," she said gravely.

"She wants to go home," said Timoken.

"Of course." Having no idea where the girl lived, Madame Magnier smiled at her.

"And you, African?" asked one of the mothers. "Where will you go, you and your camel?"

For a moment, Timoken was unable to answer her. He had given no thought to his next destination. He had no home, and he felt like a blade of grass, tossed about by the wind and having no direction. His ringed finger began to ache, and the ache spread through his body. Almost without thinking, he found himself saying, "I am going to Castile."

"Castile?" A murmur went around the table. Many had never heard of the place.

Monsieur Magnier had heard of it. "You will never get there," he said, shaking his head. "It is far, far away."

"Not too far," said Timoken. He glanced at Beri and she smiled at him.

Why had he said that name? He wondered. Castile. Where was it? He knew only that Beri lived there, and yet it seemed to tug at him. He looked at the ring, twisting it pensively around his finger.

"SHE is there," came the whisper.

"*SHE*?" gasped Timoken.

CHAPTER 14
Zobayda's Dream

Zobayda was old now and spent much of her time dreaming. There were the nightmares, too. They would always haunt her. She would see her father, in his white robes, riding out to meet the lord of the viridees, who sat on his horse like a dark shadow, waiting to kill a king. However hard she tried, she could never blot out the flash of the saber, and her father's tumbling, headless body.

Sometimes she dreamed about her journeys with Timoken, and the camel whose name she could never recall. These were the scenes that made her smile, but they always led to the day, sixty years ago, when she thought she had died, when she leaped into the river and was swept over the thundering falls. She had expected to drown, but somehow she had survived. She had tied herself to a floating log and was carried through the water for days and days. Without a doubt, any other mortal would have died, but the Alixir that Zobayda had taken for over a hundred years now kept her alive. She had been unconscious and almost dead when Ibn Jubayr, an Arab traveler, found her on the shore and saved her life. She would never forget his kind, concerned face looking down at her.

When Zobayda had recovered, Ibn Jubayr took her with him on his travels. She washed his clothes, cooked, and tidied for him. His eyes were failing and he taught her Arabic, so that she could read aloud from the large book that he always carried with him. They crossed the Mediterranean Sea to Spain, and traveled to Toledo, in the kingdom of Castile, the city that Ibn Jubayr called home. And there Zobayda met his nephew, Tariq, whom she came to love. Eventually, they were married. Her husband had died a year ago, but Zobayda still kept his workshop exactly as it had been. Tariq had made the most beautiful toys ever seen; even the king admired them, and had bought many for his children. But Zobayda could not bring herself to sell the toys that were left.

She felt unwell today. Not unwell, exactly, but troubled. The toys always soothed her, and so she descended the narrow steps to the workshop. She often walked here, her skirt whispering through the wood shavings, her fingers touching the shelves where wooden dolls sat side by side with leather animals and birds made of colored straw. She was especially fond of the camel, with its squirrel-hair eyelashes and shiny glass eyes. It stood knee-high, and when she sat down she could stroke its smooth wooden head.

She did this now, and then she took the camel onto her lap and asked it, "What was his name, that camel I rode so many years ago?" She wondered if Timoken had found a home at last. Or was he still wandering, searching for a place where he could grow old?

A sudden prick in her finger made her thrust it into her mouth. "What was that?" She examined the camel to see what could have pricked her. But there was nothing.

Zobayda had once worn a ring on the finger that was now throbbing with pain. She could still see the pale mark that it had left on her skin.

She stood up, letting the camel fall to the ground. The workshop around her began to spin and fade. Strange images swam into her head. She saw the viridees, the creatures that had forced her into the river. Now they were dressed in fine clothes, but she knew them by their strange limbs and swamp-water faces. Their powerful horses sent clouds of dust into the air as they thundered along the dry, stony road. Their leader was a boy of twelve or thirteen. He was not like them, and yet, beneath his cold, handsome face, beneath the fur-lined cloak and fine green tunic, she could see the rubbery bones and fluid sinews of a viridee.

Zobayda covered her face with her hands; the dust in her dream was so real it seemed to sting her eyes. And now she saw a great black beast, a giant horse that snorted flames and bared its teeth. It was pulling a wagon driven by a burly fellow in a brown monk's robe. Behind him in the wagon sat three others. Their faces were partially hidden by their hoods, but they were not monks. All of them wore swords in their belts, and the driver's face was scarred by knife wounds.

Why were they traveling so fast?

Now, in the very corner of her vision, something appeared that made Zobayda cry out in astonishment.

"Timoken!"

Her brother looked just as he had sixty years ago, the last time she had seen him. He was riding the camel whose name she had forgotten. Behind him came five children on horseback. They were laughing and singing, and Timoken looked carefree and happy.

"I'm glad that you are happy, Timoken." Zobayda went to the small window in the workshop, almost expecting her brother to appear on the road below.

But, of course, he was not in Toledo; he could not be. And yet she felt he was nearer than he had ever been. As she absently rubbed the mark on her finger, she began to feel that she was floating high above the world, and her brother and his friends were now tiny dots in the landscape. As they vanished from view, something appeared on the road behind them. Zobayda might have been a mile above them, but she knew that she was seeing the black horse and its wagonload of armed monks.

"Timoken, take care!" He could not hear her. Could not see her. Probably thought she was dead. There was nothing that

Zobayda could do. Besides, someone was shouting her name and banging on her door.

Zobayda's dream faded. She felt herself floating to the floor. She was back in the workshop, staring at the empty road from her small window. Somewhat unsteadily, she climbed the steps to the courtyard and went to open the door onto the street. Her friend Carmela was standing outside. She looked distraught.

"What is it?" Zobayda ushered her friend into the courtyard and closed the door behind her. "Has something happened, Carmela?"

"Didn't you hear?" Carmela lowered herself onto the stone seat in the center of the courtyard. Behind her, roses bloomed, filling the air with their fragrant scent. Carmela never failed to admire them, but today she ignored the roses and bent her head, puffing loudly.

Zobayda sat beside her friend and waited for her to get her breath back.

"Terrible news," Carmela said, patting her chest. "There has been enough fighting in our precious city, and now it is happening again. Did you not hear the shouting, Zobayda?"

"I heard nothing. I was . . . dreaming."

"Well, I heard it. It came from the river. My neighbor had the news. Strangers came over one of the bridges. They would not pay at the tollgate. When the guards forbade them entry, their leader, a mere boy so I am told, he . . ." Carmela closed her eyes. "He . . ."

Zobayda took her friend's hand. "You are distressed. Take your time, my dear."

"The boy's sword came out so fast you could not see it," Carmela cried. "Someone said he had no weapon at all. But the guard's hand was severed." She turned to Zobayda and stared into her face. "They say the boy is a sorcerer, his followers not even human."

"Not human?"

"They say they have a greenish look, arms like roots, hair like vines."

A shiver of fear ran down Zobayda's spine. "Viridees," she murmured.

Carmela frowned. "Do you know of them?"

"I have met them." Zobayda stood up and began to pace the courtyard. "What are they doing here, so far from Africa?"

"Africa?" Carmela got to her feet and made for the door. "Lock yourself in, my dear. That's my advice."

"Stay with me," begged Zobayda.

"I must be with my children," said Carmela. "Go down to your husband's workshop and stay there until it's over. They have sent for Esteban Díaz." She stepped out and closed the door behind her.

Zobayda bolted the door and pulled the bar across it. She could hear screaming now, and the clatter of hooves. "Esteban Díaz," she breathed, as she hurried down to the workshop.

Esteban Díaz was the most famous swordsman in the kingdom of Castile. He had never been beaten in a fight. Several weeks ago, his daughter had been kidnapped and Esteban had gone to search for her. But it was rumored that he was returning to Toledo, to await the ransom note that must surely be delivered.

Zobayda was tempted to look out of the window, but decided instead to sit on a bench at the far end of the room. From here she could see almost every toy, and she tried to ignore the sounds outside and think of her husband, carefully cutting and stitching, carving and painting.

The screams, the roars, and the clatter of hooves were getting louder and closer. Had the boy conjured up an army?

Zobayda waited. Waited and waited. An unlikely battle raged in the streets. If the boy was a sorcerer, what kind of dreadful power could he use against the people? But, surely, if Esteban Díaz had arrived, there could only be one outcome. Even a sorcerer could not defeat the famous swordsman of Toledo.

The sun began to sink. The toys cast long shadows on the floor. The noise outside began to fade. Silence, at last. Had the boy and his viridees left the city, or were they dead?

A sudden crash above brought Zobayda to her feet. The courtyard door had been broken. She could hear the clangs of iron on stone as the bolts and the bar hit the ground. Silence again. Zobayda waited, clutching her throat.

A figure appeared at the top of the workshop steps: a boy in a green cloak. When he descended, the viridees followed. Four of them. Their footsteps soundless, their faces sickly, their eyes red as sores. They filled the room with their awful stench.

The boy came toward her, kicking the toys out of his way. He had no use for toys. He was no ordinary boy.

"Who are you?" asked Zobayda, her mind seeing the greenish bones under his pale cheeks.

The boy's smile was icy. "My father is lord of the viridees, my mother the daughter of Count Roken of Pomerishi. I am Count Harken." He gave a mocking bow.

Zobayda glanced at the tall figures behind the boy. Her throat was dry with fear. "What do you want?" she asked huskily.

"You are awaiting your brother, no doubt. Well, so am I. We will wait together."

Timoken and the five children had been heading west for several weeks, but they were making little progress. The land was dry and rocky. Even the horses found it hard going. Sometimes Gabar would refuse to go any farther. He would sink to his knees and chew at the rough grass and thorny undergrowth, ignoring all of Timoken's attempts to move him on. There was only one way to make the camel go faster. He would have to fly.

At first, Gabar did not think much of this idea. But Timoken pointed out that there were no other camels around to embarrass him, and it was not as though he would have to fly over a mountain. So, a little reluctantly, Gabar allowed Timoken to lift him a short distance above a particularly rocky stretch of land.

The first time they saw the camel flying, the children were, momentarily, too astonished to speak, and then they all began to cheer, urging their startled horses after the flying camel.

Now, they often traveled in this way, and they began to make better progress. At night Timoken would build a fire, and they would cook the food they had managed to find during the day. When Peredur suggested they steal a chicken from one of the hamlets they passed, Timoken knew that he would have to reveal yet another of his talents.

"If we are caught, we will be hanged as thieves," Timoken told Peredur.

"We won't be caught," Peredur insisted. "How else are we going to eat? The food the Magniers gave us has all gone."

"Except for this." Timoken took the last piece of dried meat from the bag. He cupped it in his hands for a moment, and muttered a request in the language of the secret kingdom. When he spread his palms, two pieces of meat were revealed.

The others stared at the meat, and then at Timoken. No one spoke as he multiplied the meat until there was enough for all of them.

"Thank you, Magician," Mabon said at last. "We will never go hungry again." Mabon loved his food.

That evening, as they sat around the fire, Beri talked about the day she was kidnapped. She was the only one who had not yet told her story. Timoken translated her words for the others.

"My father is famous in the kingdom of Castile," said Beri. "His name is Esteban Díaz, and he is the best swordsman in the land. Whenever there is a battle, our king calls for my father. He has never lost a fight, and the king has made him very wealthy. My mother is from Catalonia, and she wanted me to marry a distant cousin who lives there. His family is rich and well connected. But my father insisted that I meet this young man first and decide for myself. And so we made a long, uncomfortable journey to Catalonia, and all the way I kept seeing two men riding behind us. Following. I told my mother, but she insisted that I was imagining it."

"And what did you decide, when you met this cousin?" asked Timoken.

Beri pouted. "I did not like him. He was older than me. Fat and boring. I ran away from him, one day. And that is when I got caught. I think that the kidnappers had followed us all the way from Toledo. They had been waiting for a chance to grab me and when they saw me alone, outside the castle, they could not believe their luck. Before I could cry out, they had run up and, while one put his hand over my mouth, the other bound my hands and feet. I was thrown over one of the horses, and they galloped off before anyone even knew that I had left the castle."

"They were not the monks, then," said Timoken.

Beri shook her head. "The monks came later. Before a ransom note could be sent, the men who kidnapped me were killed by bandits. The bandits had no idea who I was. They passed me on to another gang, who sold me to those false monks. I don't know why they kept me in a cage. I could not understand their language."

"You were wearing a very fine robe," said Timoken. "Perhaps they wanted to keep you apart from the others and try to ransom you, when they could find out who you were."

"Perhaps I stand a better chance of survival, now that I am a boy," Beri said with a grin.

The season was turning. Nights were growing chilly. When the sun went down, the sky was filled with fiery colors. For several days now, troops of soldiers had been filling the roads, and rather than pass them, the children had taken to the woods. One evening they emerged from the trees and found themselves on a wide plateau. Far below, a river wound its way through sand-colored cliffs, flowering herbs filled the air with their wonderful scent, and the setting sun made everything glow with a warm, rosy light.

They decided to stop for the night, but before he made a fire, Timoken took out the moon cloak and spread it in the sunlight.

"I believe we should arm ourselves," he told the others. "There is someone who wants the moon cloak, and your lives may be in danger, as well as mine. So I shall hide it."

Without any more explanation, Timoken began to cast a spell. Using words from the secret kingdom, he began to transform the glittering silk of the web into a soft, crimson velvet. Before their eyes the delicate threads gathered together, rippled, and spun until a fine red cloak lay at their feet.

"You shall all have one," said Timoken. "And then the moon cloak will be truly hidden."

He set about changing their, by now, ragged jerkins into warm red cloaks. He turned slim green sticks into swords, and lines of twigs into wooden shields. Later, they used charcoal from the fire to draw signs on their shields, and Timoken turned the rough shapes into fine-colored emblems: a bear for Mabon, because he was the strongest; a wolf for Peredur with his sharp, wolfish teeth; an eagle for Edern, because it was the nearest he could get to flying; and for musical Gereint, a fish from a singing stream.

"And what will you have?" Timoken asked Beri, who was deciding.

"A hare," she said at last, drawing two ears on her shield. "Because I have never been allowed to run, and I find that I love it."

For himself, Timoken chose a burning sun, the sun that had turned the moon spider's silver threads into a red velvet cloak.

When they set off the next morning, they were ready for whatever challenges they might meet. Without even discussing it, each of them knew that a challenge would very soon come their way.

It came the very next day. A passing traveler told them that they must follow the road south if they were to reach the king-dom of Castile. So they took to the road again.

Timoken was the first to feel the danger. A tremor in the earth and a distant thunder filled him with a sense of forebod-ing. He looked back and saw a cloud of dust on the road behind them. And out of the dust came the black beast and the swaying wagon with its load of brown-robed villains.

CHAPTER 15
The Black Beast

"Shall we run, or stand and fight?" Mabon had already turned his horse.

"I have a score to settle with those villains," said Peredur, brandishing his new sword.

Timoken hardly heard them. He knew what he must do. This time he did not even wave his cloak; there was no time. In the language of the secret kingdom, he called to the sky.

He was answered by a roll of thunder louder than the roar of any beast. In a second, the sky had turned an inky black and streaks of lightning flashed across the darkened landscape, striking the center of the wagon.

The wagon vanished behind a cloud of smoke, and a tall flame rose into the air. There was a distant shriek, and an acrid scent of burning filled their nostrils.

"Are they dead?" Edern looked at Timoken in awe.

"They will not follow us," Timoken replied. He could not say if the false monks were dead. He had done what he had to do. That was all.

The others cheered heartily; even Beri gave a whoop of joy. But it was too soon to celebrate. For now the black beast, untouched by the flames, walked out of the fire. Gabar trembled and gave a bleat of fear.

"Stay still, Gabar. I can stop this creature," said Timoken softly. He brought a shaft of lightning down upon the great beast's head. But still it came on. Bolts of burning light hit the creature again and again, as Timoken desperately called to the sky. He took off his cloak and swept it through the air, still calling. The lightning came down, striking the beast on every side. And still it came on.

The others had already turned their horses and were galloping away.

"The beast is possessed," shouted Edern. "It is the very devil. You can't defeat it, Timoken. Come away. NOW!"

Defeat tasted sour in Timoken's mouth. It made him afraid. But as he turned Gabar's head, he heard the beast give a bellow of surprise. The thundering hooves were still, and there came another sound, the growl of a big cat. Three growls.

Timoken looked over his shoulder. The horse had stopped in its tracks. It faced three large leopards, their bright coats glowing in the dark. It was as if they knew one another, the leopards and the horse that was not a horse. They could recognize the power and the enchantment beneath the coarse black hair and the spotted coats.

"Sun Cat! Flame Chin! Star! You have found me," breathed Timoken.

The enraged beast pawed the ground. It lowered its great head and charged at Flame Chin, who stood between his brothers. As Flame Chin twisted away, Sun Cat leaped onto the beast's lowered neck, while Star bounded onto its back. Snorting with fury, the beast tossed its head; flames from its nostrils licked Sun Cat's paws, but the leopard clung on, his claws biting deep into the beast's skull.

Timoken was aware of the other children moving up behind him.

"What are those creatures?" whispered Beri.

"Leopards," said Timoken.

"Where have they come from?" asked Edern.

"From Africa. They have always been with me."

They watched in silent amazement as the four creatures fought. Flame Chin was now braving the beast's furious kicks. One strike of those hooves would have felled him in a second. But with astonishing agility, the leopard avoided them and leaped at a kicking hind leg, biting deep into the flesh.

The beast reared up; it shook its massive head, but the leopards clung on. Suddenly, Sun Cat leaned over and sank his teeth into the black neck. The creature stumbled; it heaved a dreadful sigh and began to sink to the ground. Its groans were almost pitiful, and Timoken had to remind himself that it was not a horse, but a creature conjured up by wickedness.

The leopards did not release their grip until the beast was on its knees, its neck twisted and its nose on the ground. Star and Sun Cat slipped off the body, lifted their heads, and growled contentedly. Flame Chin withdrew his teeth from the torn leg and joined his brothers. They might have killed the beast, but they would not eat its flesh. It was not an animal, and it tasted poisonous.

"I thank you once again, my friends," said Timoken.

The leopards purred. "The thing cannot hurt you now," said Sun Cat.

"I still have far to go," said Timoken.

"We will be with you," said Flame Chin.

"Always," said Star.

The three leopards moved out of sight so swiftly it was impossible to tell in which direction they had gone.

Timoken realized that the others were staring at him. They looked bewildered.

"Can you even speak to leopards?" said Beri.

"They are friends," Timoken replied. "I am sorry if my growls frightened you."

Beri smiled. "They were very gentle growls."

Recovering his composure, Mabon said, "That fight has given me an appetite."

"For food?" said Timoken. "Let's find somewhere safe to eat." He had no need to urge Gabar down the road. The camel could not wait to get away from the fallen beast. The sun came out again. Gereint began to sing, and everyone joined in.

They found an orchard full of ripe apples. Peredur caught a rabbit, and they ate contentedly beneath the trees. That night they slept in a deserted hut. Timoken hung his cloak across the door, as was his habit now. But he was glad to know that the leopards were close.

The children decided that it would be good to work for a living. There were ripened apples in the orchards, and grapes filling the vineyards. The farmers were glad of their help and asked no questions. For their labor the children only wanted a hunk of bread and some cheese at midday, and a square meal before the sun set.

Timoken thought he should wear a turban to hide his thin gold crown. When Beri asked why he did not just remove the crown, he replied shyly that it was something he had tried all his life to do. But it was impossible.

The others attempted to pull off the crown. One by one they tugged and twisted the thin gold buried in Timoken's hair. But eventually they gave up. Edern declared that Timoken was meant to be a king, and they had better not argue with fate.

Timoken put on his turban with a resigned expression. "Edern might be right," he said. "But a king without a kingdom seems a sorry sort of person." And then he smiled, just to let them know that he really did not mind.

After several weeks, they reached the kingdom of Castile. The country had been ravaged by war, but to Beri it was home and it was beautiful. The roads were thronged with soldiers and, once again, Timoken and his friends took to the fields, to the woods, the mountains, and the wide, sandy plains.

Gabar had been quiet and gloomy ever since the incident with the black beast. And Timoken worried that, without the Alixir, the camel would suddenly become old. But after a few days walking over the sand, Gabar's mood improved considerably. He had seen other camels on the road, though he thought them a little inferior, tied one to another in a line and weighed down with provisions and weaponry. Some had almost lost their humps.

"Pathetic," he snorted, lifting his head in a superior manner and prancing forward.

"Do not belittle them," said Timoken. "They did not ask to join an army."

The soldiers were not his only worry. In spite of the bright sun, Timoken found himself caught in a mood that he could not shake off. He would laugh and sing with the others, but his heart was heavy with foreboding. It was as though a dark cloud lay between himself and the blue sky. Every day it grew worse.

Beri appeared to know the way now, but occasionally she would stop and ask for directions. Some of the villages they passed had been abandoned and destroyed, but there were people in the small, more remote hamlets. She became impatient to get home. Toledo seemed so near and yet so far. Traveling through the wilder parts of the country took far too long, she said, and she begged Timoken to take to the road again. But he would not. "I do not like soldiers," he would say.

When they finally came within sight of Toledo, they found that it was just as Beri had described: a beautiful walled city built on seven hills and almost encircled by the river. A city that shone with welcome . . . and yet . . .

"We must take the road, now," Beri cried triumphantly. "Or we will not reach any of the bridges into the city." They were on a small rise above the plain, with the road clearly visible beneath them. Beri kicked her horse and began to gallop down the hill.

"Wait, Beri!" shouted Timoken.

"What are you afraid of?" Edern asked, looking anxiously at Timoken.

"Those!" Timoken pointed to the dark shapes sitting on the city wall. There were more on the roofs, on the arches, and on the gates.

"Statues?" said Edern.

"No." The dread in Timoken's heart became heavier every second.

"Then what?" asked Edern.

"Birds," Timoken said in a low voice. "And then, not birds."

"You do not make sense." Mabon lifted a hand to shade his eyes and stared at the city. "Surely, birds cannot hurt us."

Timoken's finger burned. He looked at the ring. The eyes in the small silver face were wide with fear. A thin voice came creeping out. "Do not enter the city."

"But I must," said Timoken. "You told me that my sister, Zobayda, was there."

"I hinted," agreed the forest-jinni.

"So why should I not enter the city?"

"HE is there also," whispered the ring.

"I thought as much," Timoken said grimly.

Peredur turned his horse impatiently. "We should be following Beri, not consulting a ring," he said.

"Hush!" Timoken said abruptly. "I must know what is happening in the city."

"We shall find out soon enough." Mabon began to follow Peredur down the road, but his horse reared as a terrible scream came from the direction of the city.

Timoken urged Gabar after the others, while Edern and Gereint galloped ahead. Mabon managed to calm his horse, and came racing behind the camel.

They found Beri's horse in a small copse beside the road. A boy was holding the reins. His clothes were ragged and his face scarred by deep scratches. Beri was lying at his feet.

"What has happened here?" Timoken slipped off the camel and ran to Beri. "Did you hurt her?" He spoke in the Castilian language that he had learned from Beri.

The others dismounted and gathered around the girl on the ground.

"He — she asked what had happened," the boy said defensively. "And so I told her."

Beri began to moan. Timoken helped her to sit up and Gereint gave her his water bag. She pushed it away, covering her face with her hands. And then she began to cry. Timoken had never heard such sobbing. He thought her body might break under the weight of such terrible grief. She rocked back and forth, hardly able to breathe, as the wails and groans poured out of her.

"What happened, then?" Timoken demanded. "Speak, boy."

"The city has been invaded," said the boy. "See those birds?" He pointed to the city walls. "They did this to me." He touched his scarred forehead. "But I was lucky. Some died. A sorcerer came, and four men, who were not men . . . greenish creatures they were, things that changed and caught and tortured. The sorcerer was just a youth, but he had magic weapons: a sword that could fly, fiery stones, and a gaze that had death in it. The people ran into their houses and there they stayed. Esteban Díaz was sent for."

"Esteban Díaz?" Timoken looked at Beri.

She had no more tears left, and sat quietly staring ahead.

"Esteban Díaz is her father," Timoken murmured.

The boy hung his head. "I am sorry. I did not know that when I told her the news."

"Is he dead, then?"

The boy nodded miserably. "The bravest soldier in all Castile — maybe the world. He killed two of the creatures when they surrounded him. But the sorcerer was indestructible. And then the birds came. They were like no other birds that I have ever seen. They were not properly feathered. Their beaks were knives, their talons . . ." The boy shook his head. "They attacked Esteban from above. He had no chance. While he struck out at them, the youth ran him through — and he died."

"You saw this?" asked Timoken.

"I was hiding in a doorway, too afraid to move."

They stared at the boy. The others had come to understand a little of the language, having listened so often to Beri. There was no doubt in their minds about what had been said.

Beri seemed to be in a trance. Timoken touched her arm and said, "I am sorry, Beri. I can find no other words. But I understand your grief."

"Let us leave this place," said Mabon. "We came to Toledo to find Beri's father. Now there is no need."

"I know what you are saying!" Beri leaped to her feet, glaring at Mabon. "You want to run away, don't you? But the murderer must be punished."

The other boys shifted uncomfortably. None of them wanted to confront a sorcerer and an army of savage flying creatures. They wanted to get away from the city as fast as possible.

In spite of the forest-jinni's warning, Timoken knew he could not run away. Getting to his feet, he scanned the distant towers and spires, the tiled roofs and the tall stone walls. "Where is the sorcerer now?" he asked the boy.

"They say he went to the house of Tariq, the toy maker." The boy's gaze drifted away from Timoken. "They say he is waiting for an African — on a camel."

"Then I shall not keep him waiting," said Timoken. "You can stay here," he said to the others. "You are not bound to me, and there is no call for you to risk your lives." Without waiting for Gabar to crouch, he took a flying leap and landed in the saddle.

"But the birds," cried Edern. "How will you defeat the birds?"

Timoken smiled. "You will see."

As Gabar trotted down the hill, Timoken was already recalling the voices of the eagles he had met on his long journey. In his head, he heard the cries of falcons, of giant owls and greedy gulls, and all the birds of prey that he had ever listened to. Lifting his head, he began to call them.

Beri sprang onto her horse and began to follow Timoken. "You do not expect me to stay behind, do you?" she cried.

Gereint suddenly sang out, "I know what Timoken is doing. I too can cry like a bird. I am going to Toledo."

Edern scowled. He wished he had been the first to follow Timoken. "Come on, Peredur, Mabon. We cannot let them go without us."

And so the company of six was together when they reached the first bridge into Toledo. Their swords were drawn, their emblazoned shields hung at their sides. The wolf, the bear, the fish, the eagle, the hare, and the blazing sun. The guards had fled and the gates were open, but as the children trotted into the city, the black birds rose into the air and began to circle above them.

The city appeared to be deserted, but weeping could be heard behind the shuttered windows. The only other sounds came from the great black birds, a high-pitched, dreadful shrieking.

Timoken searched the sky for the birds he had called, but there was no sign of them.

"Only one thing for it," he said, standing on the saddle.

"Timoken, what are you doing?" cried Beri.

"I am going into battle."

Gabar grunted, "Do you want me to come with you?"

"Not this time, my family," said Timoken, laughing. His black mood had lifted and, still smiling, he sailed into the sky, his sword pointed straight at the head of the biggest bird.

CHAPTER 16
The Sign of the Serpent

The wheeling circle of birds began to close up, and Timoken found himself sailing into the center of a densely packed flock. The wind tore at his cloak, leaving his body unprotected, but the birds seemed afraid of the billowing red velvet and tilted away, shrieking with fury.

Timoken went after them, slashing at wings and talons. They soared above him and then swooped down, so fast he hardly had time to draw breath. Razor-sharp beaks tore at his turban again and again, until it unraveled and blew away in shreds, leaving his head exposed to their vicious stabs. Timoken lifted his shield over his head, but time and again, the birds knocked it away. Desperately, he kicked out at them. He lunged at the black heads and jabbed at the fiery eyes, and as he twisted and whirled he used their own language to curse and threaten them. But they still came at him, and he felt his strength begin to ebb. His sword arm ached, his head throbbed, and he found himself dropping, helplessly, lower and lower.

One of the birds swooped toward Timoken, its beak pointed at his eye; a second later a shutter snapped across his vision, and the world went black.

Covering his face with his shield arm, Timoken felt blood running across his cheeks; blood that was mixed with tears. He did not want to die before he saw his sister again. But when he drew his arm away, Timoken realized that he was not blind after all; a dark cloud had covered the sun. It seemed to fill the sky. And out of the cloud came sounds that Timoken recognized: a thousand voices, the voices of eagles and hawks, of gulls and owls, and of every bird of prey that he had ever heard. And they all spoke with one voice: "We are with you!"

The cloud fell on the black birds, covering them like a shroud; it flew around them and beneath them, until nothing could be seen of the fearful creatures. Their furious screams rose above the cries of the thousand birds of prey.

Help had come not a moment too soon. Timoken knew that he could not have defended himself any longer. The black crea-tures would have torn him to shreds. His throat was parched, his head pounded, but he managed to utter a feeble, "Thank you, my friends," before he dropped to earth.

Timoken lay where he had fallen, on the dusty road into the city. His friends rode up to him, with Gabar galloping behind.

"Is he dead?" cried Beri.

"Looks like they finished him off," said Mabon.

"No!" shouted Edern. "That cannot be."

"He looks dead," said Peredur, and Gereint agreed.

Timoken raised himself on one elbow and grinned at them. "Don't believe everything you see," he said to Peredur.

They leaped off their horses and surrounded him, cheering with relief and joy.

"You look terrible, Timoken," said Mabon.

Edern said, "Without wounds, a hero is not a hero."

"I'm not a hero yet." Timoken felt strong and confident. "Let us go into the city," he said, jumping to his feet. Gabar crouched to let him mount, and he swung himself easily into the saddle.

"You are very bloody," Beri remarked, looking at Timoken's tunic. "Do you not have a clean garment in one of those bags?" She glanced at the bundles hanging from his saddle.

"I am alive," said Timoken, raising his sword. "That is all that matters."

On the street outside the toy maker's house, the sorcerer stood watching the cloud of birds. One by one, the flying creatures that he had created with such cunning dropped like wet rags onto roofs and walls and cobblestones. A bundle of bones and black feathers fell at his feet and he stepped back. One end of his mouth curled up in a grim smile. "Well, African, a new game can begin," he muttered.

Watching from their windows, others had seen the monstrous creatures fall. Cautiously, people began to emerge onto the streets. They looked at their neighbors and shook their heads, murmuring, "Is it all over? We thought the end of the world had come."

A small procession was moving up the main street. People turned to look. They saw a boy on a camel and, behind him, five children on weary-looking horses. One of them suddenly rode up beside the camel. He — no, it was a girl — swept off her battered headgear, and a mane of golden hair tumbled out.

"I am Berenice, daughter of Esteban Díaz," cried the girl, "and I have come to avenge the death of my father. Where is the murderer?"

Someone pointed to an alley leading off the main street. Others nodded, and a woman shouted, "He is in the house of Tariq the toy maker. Tariq is dead now, but his wife still lives."

"The sorcerer keeps her prisoner," cried an old man.

"Don't go there, child," said another woman. "You cannot avenge your father. He was murdered by a sorcerer. Wait for the soldiers."

"This is Timoken." Beri pointed up at him. "He is a magician, and he has just defeated the flying creatures that have been menacing our city."

The crowd stared up at the boy on the camel. He had certainly been in a fight. His white tunic was streaked with blood, his face and hands were scarred with deep scratches. There was a glimmer of gold in his hair. Could it be a crown?

Timoken slid off the camel's back, and the others dis-mounted. Children ran forward to hold the reins. They were proud that a boy, no bigger than themselves, had defeated the flying monsters.

One of the boys pointed to the narrow street a few paces behind him. "The sorcerer and his creatures are down there," he said. "We saw them."

"Which door?" asked Timoken.

"The sign of the camel," a small girl told him.

Timoken felt the eyes of the crowd on him. He could not fail now. But before he faced the sorcerer, he had to do something about his sword and shield. They had not protected him as well as they might have. He sat on the cobblestones and laid the sword across his lap. In the language of the secret kingdom, he begged the weapon to defend him, to be invincible against all enemies, and to end the life of any being that wished him dead.

The people listened to the African's chanting. They watched in awed silence as he ran his fingers over the sword, and they saw a silver ring on the middle finger of his left hand. The ring flashed as though it were made of fire.

Timoken put his sword aside and, laying his shield over his knees, he repeated his chant. When he had finished, he asked his friends to hand him their weapons. One by one he ran his fingers over the swords and the shields with their bright emblems: the wolf and the bear, the fish and the eagle, and the running hare.

"This means that we are coming with you," said Edern, as Timoken returned his sword.

"I want it to be your choice." Timoken stood up. He glanced at Beri.

"Do you expect me to choose safety, when I have a chance to avenge my father?" she said hotly.

"No." Timoken's face was solemn.

Beri quickly tied her long hair into a knot at the back of her head. "I am ready," she said.

Timoken had been prepared to go alone, but it was good to hear his friends' footsteps close behind him. He came to a flight of steps. The door at the top was painted with the sign of a camel, and he smiled to himself. A camel could only bring good luck. But as he looked at it, the camel became a fluid thing; it turned from gold to green, the head withered and melted into the long neck. The legs vanished and the body stretched into a narrow, writhing creature: a living serpent.

Timoken mounted the steps. The others followed. He stared at the moving green coils twisting and sliding across the wood. He had never seen magic like this. His friends took a step back, but Timoken tucked his sword into its scabbard and put his fingers on the ringed door handle. As he began to turn it, the serpent's head lunged toward his hand, its open mouth reveal-ing lethal fangs. Timoken was quicker. In a flash he had seized the thing by the neck. It hissed in fury, its jaws widening, its yellow eyes glaring. But Timoken kept his grip until the serpent's mouth began to close. Its eyes rolled back into its head and it was still.

"I do not trust it," muttered Timoken, dropping the serpent to the ground.

Without hesitating, Edern pulled out his sword and cut off the serpent's head.

The others stared at it in horror. If this was the beginning of a battle, what could they expect to find behind the toy maker's door?

Timoken turned the handle and the door swung open. At first he could see nothing but an empty courtyard. There was a stone seat in the center and, behind the seat, a rosebush covered in golden yellow blooms. A breeze sent their fragrance drifting toward the group, but when they inhaled the lovely perfume, it turned sour in their nostrils and became foul and dreadful. The strength of the smell made their stomachs churn, and while they were reeling and retching about the courtyard, the petals on the bush withered and dropped. Behind the dying blooms, three shadowy figures could now be seen.

"At last!" called a voice.

Timoken shivered. It was the voice of a youth, but its tone was ancient and evil.

Someone came out of the shadows and walked around the rosebush. The youth was not much taller than Timoken. His golden-brown hair touched his shoulders, and his eyes were the color of polished green olives. Timoken instantly shifted his gaze to the hand that rested on the tip of the youth's sword. "Do not look into his eyes," he told the others.

"You know what I want." The sorcerer's smile was almost pleasant.

"The web of the last moon spider," said Timoken. "But you shall never have it."

"You could have added, 'while there is breath left in my body,'" said the youth. "And I would have answered, 'The breath in your body has not long to last.'"

"The breath in my body will last forever," said Timoken. Now that he was face-to-face with his enemy, he felt quite calm. He was aware of the two viridees, gliding around the other side of the bush, and, without turning his head, he said softly, "Be ready, my friends. Remember, your swords are invincible."

"We are ready," said Edern.

The sorcerer took a step toward Timoken. "I see you have your sister's ring," he said. "A pity she was left without it."

Timoken frowned. "What do you know of my sister?"

"I know that she lies dead in her husband's workshop."

"What?" Timoken clutched his chest. He could not breathe.

"Poor African. Did you not know that this is her house?"

Speechless with shock, Timoken shook his head.

"At least it WAS." The sorcerer's voice was filled with gleeful spite. "She would not be quiet, you see. She wanted to warn you, and whatever I did to her, she would still raise herself and shout and scream. So I had to —"

Timoken heard no more. His shriek of anguish drowned every other sound. His sword was in his hand and he was flying at the youth. Again and again he slashed at the bobbing head, but found that he was cutting through empty air. The sorcerer had become a column of smoke, a spinning green cloud. But his sword was still a weapon, and it came at Timoken in a lightning flash. Timoken raised his shield, but the youth's enchanted sword came snaking across his chest, and Timoken's movements had to become faster than seemed humanly possible. He whirled around, so that the red cloak covered every part of him except his head.

A voice cried, "I see it now! I see the web! You are wearing it, you foolish king."

But the sorcerer's sword could not penetrate the red moon cloak, and so he sent a shower of fiery stones raining down on Timoken. Most bounced harmlessly off the spellbound wood of his shield, but one of the burning stones caught the back of his neck. He staggered and fell. In a glance, he took in the fighting all about him. One of the viridees had curled its fingers around Edern's sword and pulled it out of his grasp. Before the creature could turn the sword on Edern, Beri sliced at its arm and the severed limb fell to the ground, leaving the creature gurgling with rage.

Almost too late, Timoken saw the sorcerer's blade coming at his chest. He parried the blow with his own sword, but now the whirling column came so close that Timoken could see the sorcerer's form behind the vapor. He could see the green sinews, the long fluid limbs, and the shifting, spongelike skull beneath the handsome face.

"What are you?" Timoken breathed.

"I am the only human son of Degal, lord of the viridees." The sorcerer's voice rose in triumph. "The dark blood of the forest runs in my veins, and mine is the only human heart that cannot be touched by love or the sword."

"You are not human!" cried Timoken, jumping up.

The cloud-wrapped form whirled around him, and the air hummed in its wake. Timoken turned with the cloud, bending, twisting, and leaping, as the sorcerer's sword sliced the air about him.

"And are YOU human?" screeched the sorcerer. "A boy who flies; a boy whose life depends on the web of the last moon spider?"

Timoken tried not to listen, tried to anticipate the next thrust of the sorcerer's gleaming blade, but his head was throbbing, and he wondered how long he could keep his eye on the spinning cloud.

All at once the shrouded sorcerer became very still. Timoken stared at the cloud, waiting. After such frenzied movement, its stillness was unnerving. When it came, the sword thrust was so fast, Timoken hardly saw it. How he avoided it, he would never know, but, twisting aside, he lunged at the cloud, sending his sword deep into its core, and he prayed that he had found, if not his enemy's heart, then whatever force it was that kept him alive.

For a few seconds, the cloud continued to spin, but gradually it dwindled. As it sank to the ground, a deathly wail came out of it. The sound was so terrible that Timoken had to drop his sword and cover his ears.

The viridees were nowhere to be seen, but a trail of thick green slime ran over the cobblestones at his feet. Edern was sitting on the ground with his head between his hands. When he felt Timoken's eyes on him, he looked up and grinned.

The others were all on their feet. Battered and bloody, they looked cheerfully triumphant.

"We have won, my friends!" Timoken raised his sword.

His eyes had left the cloud for only a moment, but in that time it had vanished.

"Did you see it?" he asked the others. "Where did it go?"

They shrugged, and Mabon said, "A sorcerer can vanish, you know."

Edern added quietly, "My uncle can do that — almost."

Timoken picked up the sorcerer's weapon. There were strange symbols carved into the blade: a sword made with magic, and yet the sorcerer could not take it with him.

As he studied the symbols, Timoken could see a small creature moving behind them. It was as though the bright steel were a mirror, reflecting objects that could not be seen by the human eye.

Timoken could make out the thing more clearly now. It was a serpent. The reflection of the shining creature darted up a wall;

it dropped to the ground, slithered across a street, and vanished into the shadows.

Dropping the sword, Timoken rushed to the courtyard door. He squinted into the shadows, crying, "Did you see it? Did you see it?"

Edern ran up behind him. "See what?"

"The serpent. It was small, you could have missed it."

"There are many lizards," said Edern. "They are basking on the wall. No doubt you mistook one for a serpent."

"No," Timoken said firmly. He closed the door. "It is gone now."

The others crowded around him. "Was it the sorcerer?" asked Mabon. "There's no sign of him."

"How could he vanish like that?" asked Peredur.

"He is a sorcerer," said Timoken.

Gereint looked alarmed. "Not dead, then."

Timoken shrugged. "It is likely that he has many lives. I have taken only one of them."

"Will he come back here?" asked Peredur.

"We will soon be gone," Timoken reassured him. "And then there will be nothing for him in Toledo." He noticed that Beri was sitting alone on the stone seat. She looked drained of life. Her face showed not a spark of her former bravado. She had killed a viridee, but she did not know if she had avenged her father. For where was the sorcerer now?

Timoken sat beside her. The others looked on. They wanted to celebrate, but they could not. Beri had lost her father, so how could they expect her to smile?

"You are the bravest girl that I have ever met," said Mabon. Beri was not to know that, coming from Mabon, this was an unheard-of compliment.

"It is true," agreed Edern.

"The bravest," said Gereint.

"And the most beautiful," mumbled Peredur, his cheeks reddening.

Timoken agreed with all them all, but he had nothing to add. He could only think of his sister, lying somewhere in the house. He could not believe that she was dead. She had taken the Alixir for more than a hundred years, so, surely, even a sorcerer could not end her life.

The boys' kind words failed to comfort Beri. Their sympathy tipped her over into tears again. This time she hardly made a sound. But her shoulders began to shake and a river of tears flowed down her cheeks and dripped onto her battle-stained tunic.

Timoken did not know what to do. The sight of those tears tore at his heart and he had to close his eyes. In the language of the secret kingdom, he quietly begged the sky to show Beri that, in spite of everything, the world was still beautiful.

There was a moment of silence before he felt a light touch on his shoulder.

"Rain," said Edern. "And the sun is still shining."

Timoken opened his eyes. Raindrops were falling all about them, sparkling in the sunlight. They sprinkled the creepers on the walls until every leaf held a tiny diamond. They fell into Beri's lap and splashed onto her feet. Raindrops like pearls rolled over the toes peeping out of her sandals, and the roses behind her bloomed again. Fragrant petals, as soft as silk, fluttered onto her head. Beri breathed in their perfume and smiled. "I know this place," she said.

"You know it?" said Timoken.

"My father brought me here to buy a doll."

"Where was the toy maker's workshop, Beri?"

She nodded toward an arch set into a corner of the wall.

Timoken ran to the corner. No one followed. He saw a flight of steps leading down to an arched doorway. When he looked back, he found his friends staring at him, their faces solemn and concerned.

The steps were steep, and Timoken's legs shook as he descended. He longed to see his sister again, but he was afraid of what he might find when he reached the room at the bottom.

He took a deep breath and forced himself to hurry down the last few steps. He looked through the doorway and saw a room full of toys. Sunlight came slanting through the windows, intensifying the bright colors of wooden dolls and animals. Some, he noticed, had been smashed and broken.

A woman was lying on a bench at the end of the room. Stepping carefully over the broken toys, Timoken walked toward the bench.

Zobayda lay with her hands clasped on her chest. Timoken knew that his sister was old now, but she did not look old. Her hair was black and her cheeks unlined. Her eyes were closed, but she did not look dead. He laid his ear over her heart. A faint sound reached him, the lightest whisper. But Zobayda's eyes remained closed, her hands as still as death.

"You are not dead, Zobayda," cried Timoken. "I know it. I can hear your heartbeat. Every night, for more than one hundred years, you laid under the web of the last moon spider. A sorcerer's spell could not undo that."

Pulling off the moon cloak, Timoken threw it over his sister. "Open your eyes, Zobayda," he demanded. "You are alive!"

Zobayda's lips parted and she gave a long sigh. Her eyelids fluttered and then flew open. "Timoken!" she said, and almost laughing, she sat up.

CHAPTER 17
The Golden Castle

When brother and sister came up into the courtyard they were greeted with a huge cheer. The Britons gathered around them and, one by one, were introduced to Zobayda, whose smile grew wider every second. And then she saw Beri sitting alone on the stone seat.

"And who is this?" asked Zobayda, looking at Beri.

"A brave girl who lives in Toledo," said Timoken.

"I've seen you before," said Zobayda.

"Yes." Beri got to her feet. "My father brought me here . . . to choose a doll."

"Your father." Zobayda frowned. She knew the girl now. "I'm so sorry."

"Yes. Esteban Díaz." Beri twisted her hands together. "I am happy for your . . . recovery," she told Zobayda, "but I cannot celebrate." Her eyes roamed over the group of Britons and then came to rest on Timoken. "Good-bye," she said. "I wish you luck."

Before anyone could move or speak, she stepped lightly through the door and was gone.

Only a moment after Beri's swift departure, two finely dressed gentlemen appeared in the doorway.

"The orphans told us that the menace has been defeated," said the younger man.

"Orphans?" said Timoken.

"Sadly, there are many of them in the city," said the older man. "You were unaware of them, no doubt, but they saw what happened here."

"We have come to congratulate you and to thank you." In spite of his fine clothes, the younger man had the face of an adventurer. His hair was black and curly and he wore an earring in his left ear. "I believe that one of you is — how can I put it — a magician?"

"My brother, Timoken." Zobayda proudly lifted her brother's arm.

Surprising Timoken, the two men bowed. They introduced themselves as Francisco Padilla, who was the older of the two, and Juan Pizarro. They were wealthy merchants, they explained, and would be honored to supply a feast for the magician and his friends. It would have to be a subdued affair, however, as the city was in mourning for the great and inestimably brave soldier, Esteban Díaz. Therefore, unhappily, they could not attend the feast themselves, nor could any city dignitaries. "But all of you," said Francisco, inclining his head toward the group, "all will be provided with the best food we have, attendants to wait upon you and, for each of you, a bed in my own house."

Timoken thanked Francisco. He looked forward to the feast, he said, but he would rather sleep in his sister's house, though he could not answer for his friends, the Britons.

"Britons?" said Juan Pizarro, with a puzzled frown. "They are far from home."

"They were kidnapped," said Timoken. "But they mean to return to their own country as soon as they can, and I . . ." He looked at Zobayda. "I had intended to go with them, but now . . ."

"I am not yet weary of adventure," Zobayda said curtly. "Nothing shall part us now."

By this time, the four Britons were looking quite bemused. They could only understand a few words of Castilian, and were desperate to find out what was being said. Timoken quickly translated. He could not help laughing when he spoke about the feast; his four friends' eyes widened with delight, and Mabon even rubbed his stomach.

While Timoken was translating, Juan Pizarro had been thoughtfully stroking his beard. Now he said, "I own a ship. It sails north in seven days. It carries silk and carpets to Britain. It could also carry you. But you would have to leave the city at first light tomorrow."

When Timoken told the others, they gave a loud cheer and hugged one another heartily.

"Fresh horses will be provided for you all," said Juan. "You can leave them on the dock and my man, Pedro, will bring them back."

"Thank you." Timoken hesitated before saying, "I have a camel. I cannot leave him behind."

"A camel. Ah, yes, he is being cared for in my stables." Juan frowned and stroked his beard again. "I am afraid that the captain will not allow him on the ship."

"I will persuade him," Timoken said firmly.

That evening, the five friends and Zobayda sat down to the grandest feast they could ever have imagined. There were boxes of figs; bowls of fruit the Britons had never even heard of; platters of fish, stuffed and baked; meat of every description; pickled eggs; and large green cheeses piled around crisp brown bread. And then there were bowls of almond biscuits and mounds of rich spiced cakes.

"This is even better than our prince's food," said Edern, gazing around the candlelit hall. The walls were hung with bright carpets, and the beams in the vaulted ceiling were decorated with patterns in red and gold.

"Good to have a knife and spoon again," said Gereint, who was more fastidious than his friends.

Mabon was not even bothering with his knife and spoon. He was piling food on his bronze platter and stuffing it into his mouth as though he might never eat again. The floor around him was littered with bones, and his platter surrounded by greasy bread and half-eaten fruit. He was determined to try everything.

Timoken exchanged glances with his sister, who was sitting next to him. They could both remember a time, in the secret kingdom, when they dined off golden plates and drank from goblets made of silver. And yet Timoken's mind rested on the nights he had spent with his companions, sitting together around the fire, eating the foods of the forest, with only a starlit sky for their roof. And he wondered if, perhaps, those were the best feasts of all.

When they could eat no more, and were almost falling asleep, the four Britons were shown to the beds that had been made up for them. There were two rooms with a large four-poster in each. The covers were made of linen and the curtains of heavy silk.

"We could all fit in one bed," Edern declared.

But the others decided that, for once, they would like a little more room to stretch. And because Edern did not seem to mind a squash, he was made to share with Mabon, who really should have had a bed to himself.

"I shall not sleep a wink," Edern whispered to Timoken, who had gone up to see the sleeping arrangements. "Mabon has eaten so much; I dread the noises that will come out of him."

Timoken was still laughing when he went down to join his sister.

"I always wanted children," Zobayda told her brother. "But

Tariq and I were never blessed. Now, I have five children to look after. I am very happy."

"There might have been six," said Timoken, thinking of Beri.

Before leaving, they thanked Francisco Padilla's cook for the excellent food and asked him to convey their best wishes to his master. "And one more thing," said Timoken. "There is so much food left over, will you give it to the city orphans?"

"We try to do our best for them," said the cook. "Francisco Padilla will be pleased with your request."

As they stepped out into the cool night air, Timoken said, "Zobayda, do you know where Beri lives?"

"Of course. Everyone knows. Esteban Díaz has a grand house at the top of the city."

"Will you take me there?"

"Timoken," Zobayda said gently, "no one will come to the door. The family will be in mourning."

"Take me anyway," begged Timoken.

So Zobayda led her brother up the steep streets to a large house decorated with many fine carvings. Timoken mounted the steps to the tall oak doors and knocked. No one answered. He became aware of weeping behind the thick walls. It seemed to come from every part of the building.

"Come away, Timoken," said Zobayda.

Timoken stood there a moment longer, even though he knew it was hopeless. He was unaccountably sad to think that he would never see Beri again.

"I only wanted to say good-bye," he murmured, turning reluctantly from the door.

Brother and sister had so much to tell each other, it was past midnight before they went to sleep. Within a few hours, Timoken heard a pounding on the courtyard door.

"Are you not ready?" said Edern, when Timoken's sleepy face appeared at the door. "The horses are waiting. The others are already mounted, and Juan Pizarro has provided a guide to show us the way."

"We were talking." Timoken rubbed his eyes. "Horses, you say . . ." Suddenly, he was wide awake. "But my camel — what has become of Gabar? I forgot him last night, so much was happening."

Edern grinned. "Your camel is in excellent hands. The boy we met at the gates has been caring for him."

Timoken found Zobayda throwing her possessions into a large bag.

"I cannot leave all the toys," she said. "I must take something to remind me of Tariq."

Timoken watched patiently as she rolled carved animals into her shawls and dresses. When one bag was full, she began on another. They would not be able to carry so many bundles down the street, so Timoken ran off to bring his camel up to the steps.

What a strange reunion it was. Zobayda and the camel stared at each other for what seemed like minutes before she asked, softly, "Do you think he knows me?"

Gabar appeared to be concentrating fiercely. Not a muscle moved, not a whisker twitched, not an eyelash fluttered.

"Do you remember Zobayda?" Timoken asked the camel.

"I could never forget," said Gabar.

To Zobayda, it sounded like a grunt of approval. She came down the steps until she was level with the camel's head. She kissed his nose and he nuzzled her neck. It was as if they had never been parted.

They caught up with the others on the bridge, and another long journey began.

The small procession reached the coast just in time. The ship was already loaded and due to sail the very next morning. Pedro, the guide, took a boat and carried his master's sealed letter out to the captain. He came back with good news and bad. The captain would be happy to have six children and a lady aboard, but as for a camel, that would be impossible. Camels were large, heavy, and dangerous.

"He is a very obedient camel," Timoken protested.

Pedro shook his head. "They will not take him."

Timoken looked up at Gabar. Did he understand what was being said? His expression gave nothing away. His large eyes always looked sad, his mouth always a little submissive.

"I will make sure he is well treated," said Pedro. "Juan Pizarro holds camels in high regard. He will have a good life."

Timoken led Gabar to the barn where the horses had already been stabled. He watched the camel drink deeply from the trough, and he left the barn while Gabar's back was still turned. He could not find a way to say good-bye to his companion of more than two hundred years.

There was only room for one in the tavern beside the dock. Zobayda insisted she would be quite comfortable on a bale of straw, but eventually accepted the bed, while the children went to a barn beside the stable.

Timoken did not attempt to sleep. He lay in the straw with his arms tucked behind his head, staring out at the night sky. He could hear the animals moving in the stable and he thought of Gabar.

A figure, holding a lantern, appeared in the open doorway; a small person, silhouetted against the moonlit sky.

Timoken's hand flew to the knife in his belt, but a soft voice said, "Timoken, it's me."

The others were awake now. Dangerous journeys had made light sleepers of them.

"Who is it?" called Peredur.

"It's me, Beri."

"Beri?" Timoken sat up.

The lantern was lifted, and now Timoken could see her more clearly. She was dressed as a boy again, and her hair was tucked into a leather hat.

"It's Running Hare!" cried Mabon.

"Running Hare!" echoed Gereint.

"We shall be six again," said Mabon joyfully. "The wolf and the bear, the fish and the eagle —"

"The burning sun and the running hare." Edern rolled out of his straw bed and crawled over to Timoken.

Beri came into the barn and sat beside the boys. "A friend of mine was helping in Francisco Padilla's kitchen," she said. "She heard you talking about the ship, and she came to tell me. I left the city only an hour after you. My horse is stabled and now I want nothing more than to sleep."

"But you are in mourning . . . and your mother . . ."

"I have seven brothers and sisters, enough to keep my mother company." Beri gave a huge sigh. "Soon she will try and match me up with another rich and dreary man. She will not miss me."

"I am very, very glad that you are coming." Timoken's wide smile, so white in the lantern light, made Beri laugh.

"She's coming with us," he told the others.

They gave a roar of approval, causing the horses in the stable beside them to whinny fretfully.

"Our prince likes nothing so much as a new face," said Edern. "He is always happy to receive strangers from other lands. You will be especially welcome, Timoken," he added. "And then, of course, my uncle, the magician, will be very happy. . . ."

Timoken had heard all this before, but he knew that Edern was only trying to impress upon him how welcome he would be, in that distant land over the sea.

Beri's eyes were already closing. She gave great weary yawns and flung herself into the straw at the back of the barn. She was asleep as soon as her head was down.

Timoken knew he would never sleep if he avoided the task he dreaded. He got up and crept outside. He could hear the rustle of waves on the shore. Out in the bay, the big ship was clearly visible, and he felt a shiver of excitement. He went into the stable. Gabar was crouching just inside the door, almost as if he was waiting for someone. Timoken sat beside him.

"Gabar, are you awake?"

"I am not asleep."

"I have been a coward. I could not say good-bye."

"Good-bye?" Gabar lowered his head.

"They say I cannot take you with me to Britain. We have to go on a ship, and it would not be safe for a camel."

"I understand," said Gabar. "I am just a camel. I cannot help you like the birds and the leopards. You do not need me."

"Gabar!" said Timoken in a desperate voice. "You have helped me every day of my life. Without you, I would have wanted to die."

Gabar looked at Timoken. Was that a smile? It was certainly a tear.

"What a fool I am!" cried Timoken, leaping to his feet. "I cannot leave you. I will not. We will fly together. What do you think of that?"

"I think we will fly," said Gabar.

"It is a great distance . . . over water. . . ."

Gabar tossed his head and stood up. "I am ready."

"Not now," said Timoken, and laughed.

"Soon?"

"Soon."

They settled side by side in the straw, the boy and his camel, and at last Timoken fell asleep.

The others looked worried when Timoken told them his plan the next morning.

"There's so much water to cross," said Edern. "You will fall. You will drown."

"He will not fall. He will not drown," Zobayda said. "Gabar and Timoken have traveled farther than the widest ocean. So have I, come to that."

And so it was agreed. Before Edern stepped onto the boat that would take them to the ship, he described every detail of his prince's castle. It was a golden color and the highest in western Britain. The hill where it stood was surrounded by a sea of trees. They would be red and gold at this time of year.

Timoken thought of the secret kingdom. He watched the others rowing out to the ship, and when the ship weighed anchor, he climbed onto his camel and, tugging at the rough hair on Gabar's back, he said, "Fly, Gabar, fly!"

The camel rose into the air as easily as if he were a bird. They flew above the ship, sometimes losing sight of it beneath the clouds, and sometimes skimming the water right behind it. At night they would look down and see the lanterns shining in the bow, and once Timoken saw three pairs of bright golden eyes, gazing up at him from the stern. And he caught a flash of copper red, flaming orange, and starry yellow.

"I wonder how they got on board," he said, smiling to himself.

The castle was not far from the coast, and the captain got as close as he could before putting his passengers into a boat with two strong sailors.

Timoken watched from above, as his sister and his friends climbed out onto the beach. When they began to make their way inland, he followed their progress for a while, and then he flew ahead. Soon he saw the hill rising out of the autumn trees. On top of the hill stood a castle. A golden castle in a golden sea.

"There it is, Gabar!" he cried.

"There is what, Family?"

"Home," said Timoken.

JENNY NIMMO

I was born in Windsor, Berkshire, England, and educated at boarding schools in Kent and Surrey from the age of six until I was sixteen, when I ran away from school to become a drama student/assistant stage manager with Theater South East. I graduated and acted in repertory theater in various towns and cities.

I left Britain to teach English to three Italian boys in Amalfi, Italy. On my return, I joined the BBC, first as a picture researcher, then assistant floor manager, studio manager (news), and finally director/ adaptor with *Jackanory* (a BBC storytelling program for children). I left the BBC to marry Welsh artist David Wynn-Millward and went to live in Wales in my husband's family home. We live in a very old converted water mill, and the river is constantly threatening to break in, which it has done several times in the past, most dramatically on our youngest child's first birthday. During the summer, we run a residential school of art, and I have to move my office, put down tools (typewriter and pencils), and don an apron and cook! We have three grown-up children, Myfanwy, Ianto, and Gwenhwyfar.